SECRETS
of
Karolina

KASALAINI SAUVOU

SECRETS
of
Karolína

<hr>

A NOVEL
BY

KASALAINI SAUVOU

Inks and Bindings
888-290-5218
www.inksandbindings.com
orders@inksandbindings.com

Contents

Chapter One

"There was a knock on the door. Karolina opened the door and the girl introduced herself as Savana Jones. She was there for a job interview.

"I am glad to meet you," said Karolina. "We have been expecting you, Savana."

Karolina was a beautiful woman in her 60s. Her dark hair, highlighted with grey, was braided down her back. She stood at 5ft 7inches with light blue eyes and a slender size. She took care of her husband until he died.

Karolina was still working around the house but Jasen, her middle-aged unmarried son, advertised that Karolina needed some help with laundry, ironing, cooking and cleaning in the house".

"Let me show you around the house," Karolina suggested with her warm but condescending smile. The house showcased five bedrooms with beautiful wooden floors. It had three and half baths and Jasen had his own sauna as well as Karolina. Jasen's expansive office occupied a whole wing of the house.

Savana felt an instant attraction to this handsome powerful man. Karolina abruptly swept Savana past his executive suite and said in a low tone: "Savanah, let me show you your guest bedroom."

Savana noticed that her son's bedroom was opposite from Savana's bedroom. "This is going to be your bedroom and mine is the one on the other side," Karolina said smugly. The well-appointed guest room looked out over a beautiful garden with an arbor covered in bedazzling multi- colored roses."

"My son planted all the roses," Karolina proudly said.

"So very beautiful," Savana said with a smile that belied her inner anxiety caused by her sense of being socially inferior.

"Well, when do you want to start?" Karolina asked.

"How about tomorrow morning?" she quickly replied.

"Oh, sure Savana, that will be very nice,"

"Do you have a lot of things to bring tomorrow?" Karolina asked.

"No, I don't have a lot to bring," Savana replied and then confirmed, "I will see both of you tomorrow."

Savana left them and went home to go and make herself ready for the next day.

"She looks like a nice girl," said Jasen. "Yes," "she does," said Karolina.

They both retired early that night. Karolina was very excited about the arrival of Savanna.

When morning arrived, Jasen was getting ready to go to work. Karolina fixed his lunch and gave it to him. "Oh Mama! It's eight o'clock already and I need to leave for work."

"What time is Savana supposed to be here?" he asked his mother.

"Anytime now," she replied with a growing sense of irritation.

"Okay, I will see her tonight" he said impatiently.

Jasen left for his hospital workplace and Karolina was home by herself. The doorbell rang and there was Savana. A dark cloud suddenly covered the sun and the sky threatened rain. "Well, hello!" said Karolina sarcastically. 'Being late on your first day doesn't really give me a good feeling about your commitment to responsibility! You'll meet my son later on, today."

"I am sorry I am late," Savanna confessed.

"My son was looking forward to meeting you but you'll see him tonight," Karolina said.

"Let me show you to your room." Savana took her suitcase to her room. Jasen got home about 5:30pm and Karolina already had made the dinner.

"I hope you are going to like it here, Savana!" said Jasen with his seductive smile.

I already do!" she replied, fighting back an embarrassing blush.

Savana noticed that Jasen was very good looking and then asked, "Where do you work as a doctor?"

"I am a surgeon at the Riverside Hospital which is about twenty minutes away from here," he replied.

"That is a very good hospital and it is close to home," Savana said.

After Savana cleaned up the table, she carefully put all the elegant China in the dishwasher.

Savana took a shower and told them that she was going to bed. As weeks went by, Savana was getting used to the behavior of Karolina and Jasen. She noticed that Jasen was very attracted to her but she tried to ignore his extra attention. After three months of working there, finally Jasen asked Savanna if she wanted to go to a movie and she agreed.

Savana accompanied Jasen to the movie. They went to see *The Officer and Gentleman.* She felt that Jasen liked her so she wasn't surprised to hear him whisper tenderly in her ear during the closing scene of the movie:

"I really am attracted to you Savana. You're so beautiful!"

When they arrived home, Karolina looked worried. She started to say something in Italian to Jasen but he just ignored her.

Jasen had decided that Savana should come to his bedroom while his mother was sleeping.

"When do you want to do this?" she asked breathing heavily but quietly.

"I want you tonight at midnight, Savana," Jasen said in a firm voice. Savana paused and she told him that she would see him at midnight. They had dinner with Karolina and everything was fine. Karolina went to bed at nine o'clock and Savana went right after her. Jasen stayed up until 11.p.m and then went to bed. At midnight, when Karolina was deep in her sleep, Savana got up and quickly walked to Jasen's room. Jasen made love to her right away. "Oh, Savana, I love you very much. I've never met anyone as beautiful as you. I fell in love with you the very first time I saw you," he said.

"I love you too Jasen!" she said passionately.

They made love for almost one hour. They promised each other to meet again on the following night. Savana quickly walked back to her room and went to sleep. The next morning, they both pretended nothing had happened during the night. Jasen had his breakfast and left for work.

"It is very peculiar that my son left for work early this morning-I wonder why?" Karolina inquired.

"Maybe he is doing a big operation this morning," Savana said nonchalantly.

"I think you are right Savana. "I am glad you got up early to fix his lunch. My son is very happy with you here," Karolina admitted reluctantly.

One June evening while they were having dinner, Jasen broke the news to Savana. "Mama and I will be going over to Italy next month. Mama wants to go and visit her brother."

Unable to conceal her distress, Savana whimpered, "How long are you going for?

"About three weeks," Jasen replied, "but I want you to stay and look after our mansion while we are gone."

They couldn't stay away from each other during the days leading up to his departure. They lusted for each other at least three times every week.

Savana got up one morning and she started feeling strange. She wanted to throw up and her entire body felt queasy. She made an appointment with her doctor right away. Her doctor told her the news that she was pregnant.

"Who is the lucky dad?" the doctor asked.

Savana did not respond but quickly changed back into her street clothes and left the clinic. Jasen was looking forward that night to enjoying sex with Savana again.

"How was your visit with the doctor today?" he asked her.

"I must break the news to you, Jasen, my love."

Chapter Two

"Jasen. I am going to have your baby" she purred in his ear like a pregnant cat,

"Oh, Wow! I am very happy to hear that I will finally be a father!"

"Well, I better hurry up and go to my room before Karolina gets up," sighed Savana.

She rushed off to her room, but she left so quickly that she forgot to put her panties back on. Jasen asked Savana to take him to work so she could use the car with his mother to go shopping. As soon as they left the house, Karolina decided to clean the house and make the beds before Savana came back. She thought that by doing this, they would have more time for shopping. She decided to go and do Jasen's bed first before hers.

She took everything out from the bed and to her shocking surprise she saw a pair of women's underwear. Her mind started thinking very fast. "Is my son wearing women's underwear? Is he sleeping with a woman and he does not tell me? Well, well, the only woman besides me who lives in this house is Savana. Is my son sleeping with Savana?" she asked herself. She was furious. "My son is sleeping with Savana, no! I am going to stop it!" she yelled to the empty air. But first she wanted to make sure it was Savana. She went to Savana's room and opened her dresser top drawer to check if the underwear she found in Jasen's room matched Savana's panties and sure enough -they matched.

"There are women who are better than Savana," she angrily thought. She decided to tell Jasen about her unpleasant discovery, but then she decided she was going to keep it as her secret. She heard Savana open the back door.

"Oh! Karolina, you are already dressed," Savana exclaimed.

"Yes, I have made the beds too," Karolina replied impatiently. "I want us to go shopping right away."

"Before we leave, I want to tell you something," Savana said.

"What is it?" Karolina asked.

"My boyfriend has arrived from Iraq today. He is in the military. I want to go and spend some time with him at his home. I still want to come here daily instead of living here," she spoke.

"That's fine," Karolina replied. Jasen arrived and Karolina explained to him the situation with Savana.

"Mama, that is OK." Karolina did not know that Jasen and Savana already discussed that they didn't want Karolina to know that Savana got pregnant by Jasen. They wanted Karolina to think that the baby was Savana's boyfriend's baby. One night before Savana moved out, Jasen wanted to make love to her again. He told Savana to come at the usual time which was at midnight.

Karolina excused herself saying that she was not feeling well and wanted to retire to bed early. Karolina pretended that she went to bed. Right at midnight sharp, she could see Savana from the crack of her door going to Jasen's room. She stood up and walked over to her son's bedroom. The door was closed and she could hear them having sex. She wanted to surprise them, but she didn't want to upset her son.

Savana moved back to her apartment in late June and came to work on a daily basis. Karolina noticed her stomach was big. "Are you pregnant, Savana?" Karolina asked.

"Yes," Savana answered.

"How many months?" asked Karolina.

"About two months," she answered. "Well, that's very fast work!" Karolina rudely suggested.

Karolina began to be really suspicious. Karolina didn't believe Savana that the baby's father was her boyfriend. She believed the baby's father was Jasen.

One week before they left for Italy, Jasen asked Savana if she wanted to stay at the house while they were gone. Savana replied, "Yes". "I'll call you to check on you and the baby," said Jasen.

Karolina and Jasen took the first flight to Italy that Monday. Karolina didn't say a word until they landed. They rushed their luggage to their hotel and went straight to their room to settle down.

"I better call your Uncle Angelo to say that we are here," Karolina suggested to Jasen.

Her uncle was very happy and he gave the phone to his mother. She invited them to come and have breakfast with them in the morning.

Jasen called Savana. "How are you, Savana?"

"Everything is fine," she replied.

"How many months are you now?" he asked casually but with some degree of concern.

"I'm eight months pregnant now," she said tiredly feeling the weight of her words.

"Really? Mama is very suspicious; she keeps looking at me funny," said Jasen.

Karolina asked her son Jasen to take her to her brother's vineyard in the morning. He wants us to have breakfast with him at his home and he's going to tour the vineyard with us.

"How is Savana doing? And how's the baby doing?" Karolina asked with feigned concern.

"They are both doing well," Jasen replied. She is due in a month.

"Is the baby coming that soon?" asked Karolina.

She had a big surprised look on her face. Jasen just ignored her.

The next morning arrived; they were very happy to see his Uncle Angelo. Karolina had not seen her bother for ten years.

She remembered the last time they saw each other; Karolina caught a strange virus and they had to leave right away for the states and she was admitted to the hospital.

But now they enjoyed a nice breakfast with her brother. Uncle Angelo looked seventy years old now. The Italian weather made him look strong and healthy. They spoke in Italian because neither Karolina nor Angelo spoke good English.

Karolina, always interested in the family wealth, asked her brother, "How is the vineyard and the wine business?"

"This year, I bought another 10 acres of land and I already planted grapes on it," he said.

"Uncle Angelo, how do you manage this huge vineyard?" Jasen asked.

"I will give you a tour of the vineyard very soon. We will do some wine tasting and you can meet all my employees."

"That is a very good idea," Jasen eagerly replied.

Karolina didn't say very much, but she kept on looking at Jasen and thinking about who the baby would resemble.

"I am going to wait until the baby is born and then I will confront him," Karolina plotted.

Uncle Angelo asked Jasen if he was going to marry Savana.

"No" and let's just leave it there for right now," Jasen sternly replied.

"There are many beautiful Italian women even right here in the vineyard, just let me know; I will introduce you to one," his uncle said.

"I don't think Jasen wants an Italian wife," Karolina argued to agitate Jasen.

"Yes, I want an Italian wife, mother," Jasen retorted.

Karolina stood up and left them.

The first vineyard they came to was beautiful. It sat on the hillside and it had an expansive view of the ocean.

Do the visitors come here?" Jasen asked.

"Oh, yes. Summer time is our busiest season. We usually entertain two to four hundred tourists from all over the world," his Uncle Angelo replied. "I have two restaurants right in the vineyard where people like to eat, relax, and enjoy the view of Italy."

At the first vineyard, Uncle Angelo said to Jasen, "Your mother should remember this. She used to help all the time cleaning the grapes. She hated it and she cried all the time. This is one of our oldest vineyards and your grandfather and grandmother used to work really hard to make it a successful vineyard," he told Jasen.

"Wow! Uncle Angelo, you do have some very pretty girls working for you! Maybe I should come and join you!" Jasen told his uncle.

"What is stopping you, Jasen?" asked Karolina.

"Nothing Mama!" he said irritated at his mother's need to control his responses.

"Oh! Really!" said Karolina.

He was curious because his mother was asking all these questions. He wondered if his mother already knew about Savana and their relationship. Jasen came up with an idea which involved how he would not marry Savana but how he would still take care of the baby.

His Uncle Angelo introduced him to all his employees, especially Gabriella. He made sure; Jasen met her. "Come here Jasen, I want you to meet my accountant, Gabriella!" Gabriella was a tall blonde beauty with deep green eyes the color of emeralds.

"Hi Gabriella! I'm Jasen, Angelo's nephew," Jasen said in an enticing voice.

"You are very good-looking Jasen -your uncle talks about you all the time. Are you the doctor back in America?" she asked in broken English.

"Yes, I am" he replied. "And you are a beautiful grape goddess, Gabriella!" exclaimed Jasen seductively smiling.

"Thank you," she replied with her sexy Italian accent.

Jasen kept looking at her beauty; he just could not take his eyes off her. He was overwhelmed to see such classically beautiful Italian women seemingly everywhere on his uncle's vineyard.

Chapter Three

"I am Sofia and you are?" she asked. "I am Jasen," he replied. "You must be Angelo's nephew!" she spoke. "Yes, indeed I am!" he replied in his deep masculine voice.

"What do you do here, Sofia, besides being a beautiful enhancement to the luscious grapes?" Jasen asked with a hungry sparkle in his dark eyes.

"I am one of the managers," she replied with a sweet smile.

"I should take you to dinner before I go back to the States," Jasen said, flirting again with his dazzling smile and piercing eyes. Sofia easily agreed.

Later Jasen complained to his uncle, "Uncle Angelo! now I have to choose between Gabriella or Sofia!"

"You are going to have many more exquisite choices!" his uncle replied with a gleam in his eye. His uncle Angelo took them to the next vineyard. It was Angelo's favorite. It has always been one of the most beautiful wineries to visit in the rolling hills of Tuscany- an old-world region whose country side never ceases to amaze. This was the perfect destination for honeymoons and romantic wine holidays, where the outstanding scenery overlooked endless vineyards and where the sun set gloriously each Italian evening.

Jasen was breathless observing the pastoral countryside. He had been thinking very often about moving to Italy. He was thinking about his career being a doctor, and he knew he would never be able to make money like this back in the states. He was young and he was a long way from retiring. Sitting on a wicker chair inside the winery overlooking the beautiful valley in the countryside, admiring the pretty Italian sunset, imagining the majestic Italian Alps, he enjoyed just dreaming about a future in Italy. "Come here Jasen, your mama just arrived with aunty Maria! Let's go and enjoy dinner!" Angelo said with Italian bravado.

"Where did you go?" Jasen asked Karolina.

"We went shopping in these beautiful boutiques near the ocean," said Karolina.

Maybe before we return home, we should go and buy some clothes for Savana and the baby," said Karolina.

Jasen didn't reply to his mother's question. He went inside the vine covered quaint building and sat down before the dinner was served. The waitress served them some wine and spinach pasta and marinated steak. Jasen noticed the restaurant was packed with people from different countries. He was very quiet during dinner. He noticed many pretty Italian women. Jasen was staring at one of the waitresses he found to be very attractive. He waved at her and he pretended that he wanted some water. She came back with some water and lemon and served Jasen.

"We already have water on the table," said his mother bluntly.

"I was blinded by this one's delectable beauty, so I did not see it," he told her.

He quickly asked the waitress's name and she gave it most willingly.

"Do you work here all the time?" "Yes," she replied.

She walked away from him purposely revealing her tiny waist and swinging hips.

"Jasen do you like Viola?" his Uncle Angelo asked, licking his lips sensuously.

"Why yes, Uncle Angelo! Haven't you noticed? I am a connoisseur of women and wine!" Jasen was a little tipsy, which caused him to loudly laugh at his own joke.

During lunch, there was no conversation at all. Karolina nibbled on her antipasto salad. Jasen enjoyed his appetizer of sausage-stuffed fried olives.

"Why are you so quiet Mama?" Jasen asked his mother.

"I want to enjoy my lunch," she said. I heard you were talking to your Uncle Angelo about moving to Italy," she said to Jasen.

"Yes, he first suggested that I move to Italy. I told him that I am going to think about it, long and hard," he said smiling with lust in his eyes.

"I saw those two beautiful Italian girls that he introduced you to. Have you ever thought about marrying an Italian girl?" Karolina asked.

"No, not really. I never thought about moving to Italy at all. I know it's a beautiful country and the people are nice but nothing like America," he told his mother.

"You are worried about Savana and the baby and I know why. Unless you are not telling me something," she said.

"Mama, you make me feel like I am the father of Savana's baby," he said.

"I did not say that. Why are you jumping to conclusions?" Karolina said. "Let me ask you this question: Are you in love with Savana or are you are just you using her for sex?"

That made Jasen really upset. He stood up and walked away, leaving his mother more curious about her son than ever before. It was four o'clock in the afternoon when Angelo told Karolina it was time to go back home.

Karolina and Jasen got inside the luxury SUV and started their long journey back to Angelo's Villa. The sunset was beautiful and the ocean sparkled and splashed as the waves hit the rocks on the white sandy beach. The summer breeze brought soothing warm air through the vineyards. It was refreshing to feel the salty cool breeze as they drove closer to the ocean. Angelo's villa was sitting on top of a hill and featured a great marble terrace with exotic Carrara marble fountains overlooking the endless ocean.

Angelo insisted for them to have dinner and spend the night at his house. Jasen told his uncle that they did not bring any extra clothes. Karolina suggested that he should drive back to the hotel and get their clothes. Angelo agreed. He was willing to drive Jasen to the hotel to get their clothes and come back. Jasen was willing to go with his uncle. Karolina and her sister-in-law Maria prepared dinner. On their way to the hotel, Uncle Angelo asked Jasen about Savana.

"She is the girl who is taking care of Mama and she's pregnant," said Jasen. Her boyfriend is in the army stationed in Iraq," he adroitly lied. "They lived together for a while and she got pregnant before he went back to Iraq," Jasen said, conveniently evading any more questions about Savana by stopping to exit the car. He ran quickly to their hotel room and gathered their clothes in the bag. His phone rang and It was Savana.

"Hi Savana! How are you doing?" Jasen asked.

"We are doing well. I just want to know when are you coming back home?" Savana asked lonely and impatient for Jasen's return.

"We have three more weeks to go," Jasen said. "Why did you ask that?"

"I am due the last week of next month," Savana said, slightly hurt by his lack of conscious concern for the birthing of his own baby.

"Oh! Are you really?" Jasen said. "We should be back home by then," Jasen told Savana.

"How is Italy?" she asked.

"Beautiful! My mother is enjoying it immensely.""I am going to leave now. My Uncle Angelo is waiting downstairs. We'll talk soon."

He took their bag of clothes and ran down stairs where his Uncle Angelo was waiting.

"Do you have everything? His uncle asked.

"Yes, I do," replied Jasen.

Chapter Four

When they arrived at Angelo's villa, they joined the others gathered at the table. Wine flowed freely and they enjoyed the dinner and the beautiful view of the Italian alps. Angelo told them that tomorrow they were going to tour four vineyards on the ocean side of the mountain. "You are going to see more beautiful Italian girls, Jasen," his uncle Angelo told him with a twinkle in his eyes.

Jasen's thought drifted far away as he thought about Savana and the baby. Karolina was looking at him and she knew something was bothering her son.

"What are you thinking about?" his mother asked.

"Nothing important," he replied.

"Have you heard from Savana?" Karolina asked.

"I have been thinking about her and the baby. I am going to give her another call tomorrow," Jasen said now with genuine concern.

Karolina said to herself surreptitiously: "One of these days you are going to tell me that is your baby and the biggest mistake of your life."

Jasen went to bed early that night. He was tired walking through the vineyard and meeting so many new people during the day. Savana's call made him tired too. "Good night" is all Jasen could manage to say with a weary yawn as he headed to bed.

"I asked Jasen today about Savana," Uncle Angelo addressed Karolina with brotherly interest.

"And what did he tell you?" asked Karolina.

"He just told me that she is taking care of you and she is pregnant by her boyfriend who is stationed in Iraq," Angelo told Karolina.

"I am going to share my secret with both of you and you must not tell anyone including my son," she said. "What is the secret?" her brother Angelo asked.

"Jasen hired Savana to come take care of me. She moved in with us to make it easy for her. But it so happens that she would go to Jasen's bedroom at midnight and allow Jasen to make love to her. Her bedroom is right next to Jasen's room. This had been going on for two months until one day while I was making the bed, I saw girl's panties on top of his bed. I was surprised and curious and asked myself so many questions.

"Who is sleeping with my son?" I did not see any woman coming to this house. The only woman who is living in this house is Savana. He could find someone better. But this secret is still growing in darkness within me. I was going to confront him while we were here. But I changed my mind. I will wait until the baby is born. That is my secret" Karolina said.

"Jasen didn't know all this time that you knew?" her brother asked.

"He is very suspicious of me and he knew that I am up to something. However, he has not asked me yet," Karolina explained.

"Do you think he will marry an Italian or American girl?"

"He would only marry Savana for the baby's sake, but I don't think he will marry her." said Karolina. "He wants to take out one of the girls he met yesterday. Gabriella is a beautiful blonde with green eyes, but he was not really attracted to her."

"Maybe later on," Angelo said hopefully.

Uncle Angelo told Karolina that Jasen was also going out with Sofia, and that he would be dining with Sofia this evening. Jasen confided to his uncle that Sofia is an Italian beauty, a brunette with blue eyes and tall long legs." Karolina replied vindictively, "I hope he is not going to fall in love with her!"

When Jasen overheard his mother's remark, he said: "Oh! Mama", why don't you just try to be nice for a change?"

"Remember you still have Savana back home and she's ready to have her baby," warned Karolina.

"I am not worried about Savana, and you sure are trying to ruin my dinner tonight!" he replied impetuously. Jasen left to go and meet Sofia. She was wearing an elegant flowing light blue silk sundress. They greeted each other and went inside the restaurant and sat down at the table. "You look very beautiful tonight, Sofia, your dress matches the pretty azure color of your eyes and the ocean!"

"Thank you, Jasen, you look quite handsome too," said Sofia. "When are you going back to America?" she asked.

"We have less than a month before we fly back," replied Jasen. They said good night and went home. Jasen kept thinking about Sofia and he was beginning to fall in love with her. He kept thinking about her and he thought about Savana with the unborn baby. He decided he was going to talk to Savana when they arrived home. He would tell her that he was calling off the wedding but he was going to support the baby. While he was deep in thought, Karolina showed up.

"You look confused my son; do you like Sofia?" his mother asked.

"No Mama! I know what I want- just leave me alone!" yelled Jasen.

He really liked Sofia. The next day he asked Sofia out to dinner. They enjoyed al fresco dining at this elegant restaurant near the winery. Sofia really looked beautiful. When she smiled at Jasen her blue eyes, which matched the color of her dress, sparkled and drew Jasen deep into her soul like the azure Mediterranean Sea.

Jasen was mesmerized and knew he was going to ask her out again before they left for the states. The next morning his mother asked about his dinner with Sofia.

"It was very nice," Jasen answered curtly annoyed at his mother's probing.

His uncle Angelo came to tell them that tomorrow they would visit one of his favorite wineries.

"It is the biggest destination for many couples celebrating their honeymoon or desiring a romantic wine holiday. Imagine a winery featuring outstanding scenery overlooking endless vineyards where the sun sets each glorious Italian evening. We have beautiful women working there too, Jasen."

"You should not mention women to my son! Women are his wackiness," said Karolina. Her brother just laughed at his sister.

Jasen sat outside the winery admiring the beautiful scenery. He thought about how God chose him to be a doctor so he could help and heal people. He was thinking of Savana and the baby. She would really love to see all the Italian vineyard and wineries.

He decided to call Savana and see how she and the baby were doing. She was happy to hear from Jasen. "I am doing very well and I only have one month to go before I have your baby!" she spoke excitedly.

We are coming home in three weeks and we can talk some more then," said Jasen.

They said good bye and hung up. Jasen was really thinking hard now if he was going to break the news of possibly moving to Savana. While he was deep in his thought, his mother showed up and sat beside him.

"I just talked to Savana and she told me that she is due next month. I told her that we are coming home in three weeks," he told his mother.

"Is she okay and the baby?" asked Karolina. "Yes," replied Jasen.

"I am going shopping with your aunty Maria. What are you going to do today?" Karolina asked her son.

"I am going to hang out with uncle Angelo and maybe I will tour the vineyard with him. It is very huge. I think it is going to take the whole day," he told Karolina.

"That's going to be very good for you. Your uncle is a very good business man. He can teach you a lot of exciting things about how to start a winery business," said his mother.

"Yes Mama, I hear you," said Jasen.

"I see you have been thinking a lot about your life and I am worried about you my son".

"Don't worry about me, Mama, I am a grown man and I can make my own decisions," he told his mother. "I am going to take another trip to Italy after Savana has the baby."

"I see a lot of secrets around here," she said.

"That is very true. You can just feel it," Jasen said.

"Do you have a secret, Jasen?" asked Karolina

"Why do you ask me that question, Mama?" asked Jasen. "Do you know something about Sofia that you haven't told me about?" Jasen asked Karolina.

"I see that you really like Sofia," said his mother.

"Yes, I do she is a rare beauty to me. There is something about her that I really like. Gabriella was beautiful too but I prefer Sofia," he confided.

"Okay, Jasen your aunty Maria is here and we will continue this conversation later."

"Have fun shopping!" Jasen said to his mother.

His uncle arrived and asked Jasen if he wanted to have a ride down in the valley with him. He just nodded his head.

"I noticed that your mother was talking to you for a while there."

"Yes", Jasen replied in a near whisper. 'She was telling me that these wineries have so many secrets."

"Yes, she's right," said Angelo.

"Can you tell some of them?" "I will tell you one well known one that your mother should have remembered very well. She was only twenty years old.

The story was about an Italian baron who was very wealthy and had many wineries. He was single. He always entertained many beautiful Italian women and mainly they were commoners involved on an unforgettable journey with an aristocrat. He had ten Dover guard dogs. They slept with him at night. He was taking drugs- cocaine mainly. He got to the point that he was sleeping with prostitutes and paid them a lot of money. One day he decided to take a trip to America in Hollywood. The house in the Hollywood hills over looked the city and the ocean. When he arrived there, he was doing the same thing all over again-drugs, prostitutes, even having illicit affairs with celebrities. He had lived there for fifteen years when he received a call from some woman that he used to date that he had made her pregnant on their last date. He didn't believe her. He met a psychic in Los Angeles who he hired to help him know the truth. She happened to be Greek. She practiced hypnosis and so she hypnotized him and he revealed his secret stories of corruption and consequences.

She told him someone was plotting to kill him because he made his wife pregnant. They had been looking for him for years. She told him they showed her his death. When he had been carried to the church for his funeral, every boy was wearing black. She saw this one particular vineyard where so many workers were killed because they were having sex with someone's husband or wife. She told him that she saw him. He did not sleep with women inside his house, but instead he took them to the winery and made love with them there. Sometimes he would take them to the vineyard and make love to them among the grape vines. She asked if the story was true and he agreed.

"You have some dark stories and some that you are afraid to tell anyone, even while hypnotized."

"That is very true. I am afraid to tell it to anyone because they will silence me forever."

Chapter Five

"I want to go back to Italy and see my ancestral villa and my winery and my friends," the baron pleaded. "And what is stopping you?" the psychic asked.

"Someone is going to kill me!" he cried. "I did horrible things-unspeakable acts- against women!"

What I did to these women was sad," the baron confessed. "I made love with all these commoners who were beautiful but I would not marry any of them. I would sleep with them and let them go. Until one of them got pregnant. Then I discovered her secret. She happened to be nobility who was married to the king of Italy's cousin. I really loved her in spite of our adultery. We would meet in secret in the vineyard and make love. She would rush quickly home before her husband got home I come back home quickly before he caught both of us. I could not take her to my house because everyone would know she was committing adultery with me. I decided to just stop seeing her. She was two months pregnant."

Her husband knew that was not his baby. She wouldn't tell him the name of the man. He fled to America. He knew If he returned to Italy, they would kill both of them. The baron lived in America fourteen years trying to escape his sordid past. When he decided to come back home, his illegitimate son had grown up, and he was looking for his father. His mother told him who his father was. When he was preparing to go and see his father, he was told that his mother and the baron were murdered.

Jasen was shaken by this story of the consequences of lustful attraction.

"Uncle Angelo, it is sad they were both killed. He tried to deny the paternity of his baby but he loved him very much and he didn't want to deny him."

"This tragic story was well known here in Italy," Angelo said. When royal blood lines became compromised, so did the rightful inheritance of wealth and power become threatened."

"We better go back to the winery to see your mama and your aunty Maria. They will be wondering where we are," said his uncle.

"There you are!" said Karolina. "We were wondering where you went."

"Let us go and have dinner," said Angelo.

"Your Aunty Maria took me to these beautiful boutiques near the ocean. The ocean is just beautiful! You should come with us before we return home. I want to get some clothes for Savana and the baby," said Karolina.

"I just have too many things on my mind, Mama," said Jasen.

"What has been bothering you?" asked Karolina.

"I am thinking of moving to Italy," said Jasen. "Italy is a beautiful country and you can have a business here and live very well. I am glad that I speak fluent Italian otherwise I would never move here."

"What are you going to do with me?" his mother asked, fearful of ever losing control over her only son.

"I don't know Mama- that's up to you," said Jasen.

"Uncle Angelo told me this secret tale about this baron who slept with all these commoners and married women. He did not take them to his house but took them to the winery or vineyard. He was seriously involved with the king of Italy's brother's wife and made her pregnant. He left Italy and fled to America. Many years later, he decided to return to Italy. The husband knew about it. One night they were sleeping together again, and her husband killed both of them while they were asleep," recounted Jasen with genuine horror at such happenings.

"That's a true story. I was very young when that incident took place," said Karolina. "It is a good lesson for unfaithful cheaters," she said.

"How many more secrets do you know Mama?" asked her son.

"This was well known. I know many secrets; however, I cannot tell all of them right now," she said. "Your uncle Angelo needs to tell you one more story," said Karolina. Angela tells it better than I can," she said.

"Uncle Angelo is calling us. The dinner must be ready," said Jasen.

Jasen saw this beautiful waitress serving their foods. He wanted to communicate with her. His Uncle Angelo was looking at him with a grin on his face. Jasen was flirting with her. He took her name and phone number and told her that he would give her a call. The next day, he went shopping with his mother. They bought some clothes for Savana and the baby. Karolina was watching her son shopping.

"You do care for Savana, Jasen," said his mother.

"Yes, I do care for Savana and the baby. She is going to have her baby in two weeks," said Jasen.

"Are you excited about the baby?" his mother asked.

"Of course, because I am looking forward to seeing the baby. Savana is part of our family. This has been a good visit," said Jasen.

Karolina and Jasen spent their last night at her brother's house. They talked most of the night sipping on cappuccino and enjoying tiramisu and then went to bed late. The next day they all got up and walked down to beach. The ocean was beautiful. The white sandy beach with the tides rocked the beach. They went to have breakfast in one of the oldest restaurants in Tuscany. It reminded Karolina and Angelo about their parents who used to take them when they were little to a restaurant up in the picturesque mountains in Lucca. The breakfast was delicious and the restaurant was sitting at the edge of the ocean looking out on the simple fishing boats painted aqua blue and white. The water was so clear they could see the tiniest fish swimming among the colored rocks.

"I am coming back here for Christmas," said Jasen.

"Great! We would love to have you back!" exclaimed his uncle Angelo.

"I want to check out some of these wineries that are on sale right now. You can help me choose the right one," Jasen said.

"Is there any particular one you are interested in?" his uncle asked.

"The one up on the hill from yours," said Jasen.

"That's a good vineyard. The Ferraris, the owners have moved to Switzerland. Mr. John Ferrari has decided to sell it."

"That is the one I want to buy!" Jasen replied enthusiastically.

"Have you tried to contact them?" his uncle Angelo asked.

"Yes, yesterday and they want to meet with me."

I told him that I am here right now, and I will go back to America in two weeks. I asked him if he knows you and Mama. He asked me if my mother was Karolina. I told him yes. He said he basically grew up with you and Mama. He was really happy to talk with me. He is coming over this weekend to see Mama.

"I am glad that you are doing this. He is going to give you a very good price," his uncle said.

"I am planning to move here," Jasen said with conviction.

"What are you going to do with your mother?" asked his uncle.

"She always wants to come back here and live. I always tell her maybe, one day, we will. I haven't told her that Mr. Ferrari is coming this weekend," Jasen said.

"How soon will you be moving to Italy?" His uncle asked.

"The end of the summer next year but I will be traveling back and forth for a while." said Jasen. "We will start packing as soon we get home.

John Ferrari arrived at 11 a.m. on Saturday morning. He stayed in a quaint village hotel. Jasen and his uncle went to see him to enjoy conversation and al fresco dining. John was a very pleasant man and he was happy to see Angelo. They talked about the price of the vineyard. He gave them a very reasonable price and Jasen was very happy about it. Jasen was prepared to buy this old vineyard with varietal grapes found nowhere else in Italy. The next day his uncle and he were going to join John who planned to show them the winery. Jasen was very excited about it. On their way home, his uncle Angelo told him that he was really happy about the choice he made. He could envision large family gatherings on the vineyard's palatial terrace.

When they got home, Karolina and Maria were still up. "There you are, how was Ferrari?" Karolina asked.

"He looked good and he was very excited to see us at the winery and to give us a tour of the vineyard as well," Angelo told her."

"Oh, Jasen!" Karolina said with adulation and pride in her voice. "You have made a perfect choice to buy the vineyard and the winery with its elegant wine tasting rooms. We grew up with the Ferraris. We used to go to school together. Our parents on the Rossi side of the family, used to be his parents' best friends. I was going to marry him but your father was very fast to grab me," Karolina said jokingly. Then with sadness, she added, "Of course that was before your father mysteriously died in America."

"He told me about you but he didn't tell me that part," said Jasen.

"Well, I am very proud of my son that you are purchasing this heritage vineyard as a new business venture!" Karolina quickly added.

The next day they prepared to go and meet John. "I want to come too. I want to see him again," Karolina opined.

"Of course, Mama, he will want to see you too," said Jasen.

They drove up to the mountain where the vineyard was located. John was very happy to greet them. He embraced Karolina and told her that she had aged with beauty like his finest wine.

"I am glad to see you again Karolina," said John.

"Yes, it so nice to see you again," said Karolina.

"You have a very smart son and he is very cultured like you," John added.

They all sat down at an antique carved wooden table overlooking the mountain where the vineyard scenery was breathtaking. It was very beautiful and Karolina remarked that she could hear the ocean roar from afar. John reported that the vineyard and winery had eight hundred employees. Jasen said he planned to increase the number of workers after he purchased this unique property. John and Jasen negotiated the deal and Jasen bought the vineyard. His mother was very happy that he made an excellent deal with John.

They all went with John to his private wine cellar to celebrate the deal. They talked about the many secrets the vineyard holds. John even brought up one of the secrets his parents told him about these two married couples who were having an affair. They kept the secrets for a long time. They hid it pretty tight until one day someone saw them; she did not quite see their faces but noticed something very strange about them. The woman looked very familiar to her. She was somebody else's wife. She was hiding her face all the time until that day. This winery worker kept her knowledge of this secret affair to herself for a very long time. Until one day, a man came and ate at the restaurant in the vineyard. She overheard him saying that he saw a horrible killing in the vineyard. The murderer took the body and buried it in the newly planted grapevines. It was said that the merlot and chianti grapes turned an intense blood red color. He could not remember exactly where the cheating lover was buried because the vine had grown so big. He said this man must be the man who was sleeping with the wife of the man that killed his lover. That was the first love affair that happened in this vineyard.

There were many different stories," said John.

"Don't scare me!" Jasen said.

"I am not scaring you because these are true stories. The funny thing is they always choose the vineyard or winery for their affair," John reported. "You know why they choose this kind of place?

"Because no one can see them or find out who they are," said Jasen.

"Your mother knows many secrets," said John Ferrari.

"Yes, I do. I know many secrets and I haven't told many of them to Jasen," said Karolina.

In the fresh dew of the morning, they went to see the winery and the restaurant. Angelo wanted to introduce Jasen to the workers. Jasen was very excited and happy. This day was a celebratory day when Jasen would officially own the vineyard.

They went and met all the workers both women and men and learned of their particular responsibility in the vineyard and the winery. Jasen was very lucky that he spoke fluent Italian because all the employees did not know the English language. He was very happy to meet his future laborers who were almost the same age as him. He checked out the restaurant and he noticed that it needed some renovation, and the winery needed renovation as well. He noticed that most of the equipment that they used in the winery was very old. He hired an experienced builder of wineries to check on all the things that needed to be replaced.

Jasen had a lot of work in front of him, and he and his mother had only one week left before they returned to America. Now he faced the biggest secret he had been hiding from his mother. Savana and the baby! John returned to Switzerland. They promised that they were going to come to Tuscany every year. Jasen tried to finish all the paper work and the payroll as well. His uncle Angelo was going to take care of the vineyard for him until he sorted out everything needed for Savana and the baby. He was planning to return to Italy in the fall.

Jasen and Karolina started packing their clothes and three cases of wine for his uncle to send later on. The following Wednesday, they took the first flight to America. They said goodbye to his uncle Angelo and his wife Maria. They said they would return in the fall of next year.

Back in America, Savana was happy to know that Jasen and Karolina were on their way home in time for the baby's arrival. Karolina was looking forward to seeing Savana especially when she was going to give birth in a few days. She wanted to see how her son Jasen would react to reveal emotions that the baby was his. Jasen would not go back to work as a doctor, but he was excited to tell them the good news about the vineyard he had just bought in Italy. He was planning to give his resignation to the hospital very soon. Savana was glad to see Jasen and Karolina. They were happy to see Savana.

"Looks like the baby is going to come out any minute now," said Jasen.

"Are you excited Savanna that the baby is going to be born any time now?" asked Karolina.

"Oh yes," exclaimed Savana.

Karolina unpacked and wrapped all the presents for Savana and the baby while Jasen just stared at Savana for a very long time noticing her maternal beauty and glow. Jasen was really in love with her. He missed her while he was in Italy. Even though he had met all those beautiful Italian girls, there was something very special about Savana. She was carrying his baby.

Savana abruptly broke Jasen's musing with a loud shocking scream of pain.

Labor had begun in earnest. They rushed to the hospital. As soon as they got there, Savana had a beautiful baby boy who weighed seven pounds and six ounces and measured about twenty-one inches. Momentarily, the miracle of birth had opened Heaven and poured down God's love.

Jasen was very excited and happy to see the baby. He could see the baby resembled him. Savana and the baby had to stay one more day before they could go home.

"I better go home and bring Mama in to see the baby! I just can't wait to see her reaction," Jasen told Savana. Savana was exhausted from the delivery but she still gave Jasen a big grin in agreement.

"How is the baby my son?" asked Karolina breathlessly when she arrived at the hospital in record time.

"Well Mama, I can't tell and the baby is too small to tell," said Jasen smiling as a proud father from ear to ear.

Karolina did not want to embarrass her son. She asked him the name of the baby.

"I am going to name him Jerry named after my brother who died," said Jasen.

They went straight to the maternity ward and there the beautiful baby slept peacefully. They were just waiting for Jasen to take them home. Karolina was happy to see the baby. Karolina asked Savana if she could hold the baby. Savana gave her the baby to hold. Karolina took one look at the baby and she could see that he just looked like

Jasen. She did not want to say anything to her son. They arrived home. Karolina already had prepared the room for the baby.

"We are going to name the baby "Jerry" which was my brother's name," Jasen told Savana.

She was very happy about it. They went to sleep that night. Jasen was thinking about Savana if should marry her or not. He wanted to take them with him to Italy. But he could not go to sleep at all. He got up early to peep at the baby. He went to the baby's room, and there was Savana feeding the baby, "Oh Savana, I missed you so much. I was thinking about you all the time I was in Italy," he said. I missed making love to you. He kissed Savana very passionately and he held the baby. The baby cried and Karolina heard the baby crying. She rushed to the baby's room and to her surprise, she saw both of them were there with the baby.

"What are you doing here my son?" she asked.

"I could not go sleep last night so I decided to come and see the baby and I saw Savana feeding Jerry," said Jasen.

Karolina did not respond to Jasen but instead turned to Savana and observed her exhausted demeanor.

"Savana you must be very tired," Karolina observed with some warmth.

"Yes, I am," she said. "Having a baby is a big ordeal. I never experienced anything like it. Carrying the baby for nine months was hard enough," said Savana. "I don't think I want to have another baby!" she said.

The baby was growing big and he looked more like Jasen every day. Jasen could not hide it from his mother anymore. He waited for his mother to ask him about the baby but she had not commented so he assumed that she was not going to ask him right now.

"I am going to baby sit for Jerry today while Savana goes to the doctor for a checkup," said Karolina.

Jasen heard her and thought this would be a perfect time to talk with his mother. Karolina went to check on Jerry and to her surprise, she saw Jasen was holding Jerry.

"Well, well funny that I see you in here," said Karolina acting surprised.

"I could not go to sleep at all last night. I have a lot on my mind and I feel like I have to make a decision right now about Savana and the baby," explained Jasen. "I really love this baby, Mama, and I love Savana too. I am thinking of taking them with me to Italy!"

"I want to ask you a question about baby Jerry. "Are you his father?" asked Karolina without emotion and in a rather accusatory tone. Jasen just broke down and cried.

"Yes, Mama, he is my son. Now I am looking at him, I do not want to leave him. He is a very beautiful little boy," cried Jasen.

"I am glad we talked about this. I've known it all along that he is your baby. But I did not want to confront you or embrace you. I know time will tell," said Karolina. How did you know?" Jasen asked his mother.

"I knew it was your baby. I noticed you had changed a lot. While we were in Italy, you were calling Savana all the time. Now, the result, Savana gave birth to your baby. The good news is you have a beautiful baby and Savana is very pretty and young and I am happy even though it was a secret love child," spoke Karolina in a hushed and hurt tone of voice.

"I am very sorry Mama that I lied to you and try to understand, that when I first met Savana, I fell in love with her right away and I have always wanted a child and if I told you all that you would have been very upset because you always wanted me to marry an Italian woman. I have decided not to marry Savana and instead they will come with us to Italy when it is time to move," said Jasen.

Karolina agreed to his decision. They both heard Savana open the back door and they both stood up to greet her.

"It is very nice to see both of you here," said Savana.

"We both went to watch over Jerry. He is a happy baby and a beautiful boy," said Karolina.

Jasen looked at Savana and saw how glowing and beautiful she was-like a Renaissance "Madonna with Baby" painting by Raphael. He wanted to make love to her and tell her how much he loved her. But he knew he should hold off with his physical amour for a while until Jerry got bigger. Karolina cooked pasta and fish for dinner and they all had dinner and they talked about their trip to Italy. Jasen broke the news to Savana that he told his mother about the baby. Savana was happy. She felt that finally Karolina would know the truth that she was his grandmother.

"I am going to tell you more exciting news, Savana!" Jason said exploding with excitement. "I just bought a vineyard in Italy and we are all going to be moving to Italy," said Jasen the proud father.

"Wow! Now, I am going to see Italy! When are we moving?" she asked.

"Next year or sooner," Jasen spoke.

"Great! Jerry will be almost two," said Savana.

"You and Mama should start packing now. We need to get rid of the stuff we do not need,"

The baby was almost one year now and he was beginning to walk. That was the happiest moment for Jasen to see his beautiful son start walking. He looked at Savana's beauty and he knew he had made the right choice for her to have his baby. He started to make love again to Savana and she missed him very much. He told Savana that he missed her a lot too and now that his mother knew the whole story, they could both relax and be happy.

But Karolina was always suspicious of Savana. She felt that Savana was hiding something. She had not been honest to Jasen. She wanted to talk to her son about it.

When Savana went shopping and she asked Karolina to look after Jerry, Karolina figured this would be a good time to talk to Jasen.

"There you are. I have been looking for you. Where is Savana, Mama?" asked Jasen.

"She went shopping" Karolina replied.

"Savana needs to spend more time with Jerry instead of going out all the time," Jasen told his mother.

"There is something I want to tell you. I have been watching her and I feel that she has a secret. After she had Jerry, she started to go out all the time and did you notice she would go for a very long time?" questioned his mother. "The next time she goes out you should follow her or have your cousin Tom to follow her. He is a detective and I am sure he will do that for you," said Karolina.

Jasen agreed and called his cousin Tom right away.

Chapter Eight

"Remember my suspicion from the beginning about her was right. There was something about Savana this time that is really strange," said Karolina.

Tom showed up right away. They had not seen each other for a while. "What's up Jasen, I heard you have a baby boy," shouted Tom.

"Yes, I am a proud father!" replied Jasen. "I want to tell you about Savana the mother of my child."

After she had the baby, she kept going out and she would tell us she had a doctor's appointment or go shopping all the time and today she's disappeared again. "Mama was very suspicious of her from the beginning. What do you think, Tom?" asked Jasen.

"What I am going to tell both of you is not going to be very good news. Usually when women do this that means they are seeing another man."

"How old is Savana?" Tom asked.

"Twenty-two," replied Jasen.

"I am going to do this for you and see, if she is secretly seeing some body. Is she still out?" Tom asked. Jasen nodded his head in the affirmative. "I am going to check her out and I will get back to you," Tom said.

The first place Tom went looking was the shopping mall. He looked around the mall and went upstairs. He did not find her. He decided to sit down on a public chair in the mall and just watch people walk by. He was sitting straight across from the California Grill restaurant. He checked his watch and saw it was after one o'clock. He became very surprised when he saw Savana and another man. They came out from the restaurant and walked straight to the parking lot. Tom stood up and followed them. They both got in the car together and drove off. Tom was following them. He kept on following them until they got to East Sacramento. He saw her car was parked at this man's house.

The man looked respectable, like he had a very good job. He saw them go inside the house and they closed the door behind them. He waited until she came out. He noticed the house was not far away from Jasen's house. He took down the address of this man. He called Jasen and told him the news.

"Savana has been having an affair with a man," his cousin Tom told him. He told him the address of this interloper and Jasen knew him right away.

"I know this man! He just recently divorced and he is a doctor," Jasen said. "I already made up my mind in Italy that I was not going to marry her but that I would just take care of her son. Now I am going to fight for custody of the baby," said Jasen bitterly.

"This is my advice to you, do not keep her at your house," said his cousin.

"What about the baby?" Jasen asked.

"How old is the baby?" Tom asked.

"He is almost three now," said Jasen.

"Aunt Karolina can take care of him now," Tom replied.

"Of course, she can.

Start the custody battle right away before you move to Italy," said his cousin. Jasen called another cousin who practiced family law to come and meet with him at his house right way.

His cousin the lawyer arrived. "Hi Jack," said Jasen.

"This must be really very serious that you called me like this, "Jack said.

"Yes, it is very serious and I need your help," said Jasen. "You know, I have a baby now. I am going to tell you the story later. The girl that came to care for Mama ended up sleeping with me and she got pregnant. Now she has my baby boy and he has grown up. He is three years old now." "I found out today that she has been having an affair with this doctor living down the street from here. I think this must have started while we were in Italy. But she was pregnant then. Now I want to have custody of the child. After the baby was born, we noticed that she always wanted to go out all the time. She would be gone for two to four hours. But Mama was watching her all the time. "That was the first time for Mama to tell me about Savana's secret behavior. I had decided to marry Savana. I am going to move back to Italy this summer and I already told Savana that she is coming with us and then this happened," said Jasen.

"Are you going to allow her to stay here?" asked Jack. "I will go ahead and file the custody papers now."

"Let her stay here until we finish filing the papers and then we can take the next step," said the lawyer.

Jasen was thinking very hard what to do with Savana. He lost his trust in her and he wanted her to leave. Savana still had her apartment. He was going to talk to Savana about moving back to her apartment.

Chapter
Nine

But what if she wanted to take the baby with her when she moved back to her apartment? Jasen was hurt and confused and struggled with these tormenting questions.

He did not want to pull the trigger yet. Savana returned from her shopping trip. She went to see Jerry and he was with Karolina. Jerry was happy to see his mother and ran to her open arms.

"Did you have a nice shopping day?" Karolina asked.

"Yes, I did" she replied.

Jasen just ignored her. Savana, noticed that Karolina and Jasen did not talk very much to her. While they ate dinner, Jasen was very quiet. He stood up and went to watch the news. Karolina put all the dirty dishes away and left to join her son. After Savana put Jerry to bed, she went and took a shower and went to bed.

Jasen told his mother what was going on. Karolina was not surprised at all.

"I knew she was doing something. She has been going out for a very long time. She had a doctor's appointment one after the other.

Surprisingly enough, she was sleeping with that doctor and she did not even care about her baby," Karolina said.

Jasen surmised that Savana was having an affair with this doctor right after she had the baby. He asked some of the neighbors if they saw her around. One neighbor watched her all the time coming to the doctor's house. Sometimes in the morning and sometimes in the afternoon. One day the neighbor saw her spending the night there. She had been having an affair with this other doctor for two years.

"Are you sure this is your baby?" the lawyer asked Jasen. "Oh yes, Tom. Jerry is a carbon copy of me."

"You should ask Savana first before you get rid of her," said Tom.

"I am going to file the custody papers first then I will talk to her. In the meantime, I am going to let her stay here for Jerry's sake."

The lawyer called Jasen to remind him that his custody trial was next month. Jasen told him that Savana was still living there.

What am I going to do with her?" asked Jasen. The lawyer told him to talk with Savana and explain to her what's going on." "I will do that today," said Jasen.

He talked to his mother about it and she was okay with it. He called Savana and Karolina to the sitting room because he wanted to talk to both of them.

Jasen broke the news to Savana.

"I want you to be honest with me with what I am going to ask you, Savana."

"Are you having an affair with someone?" Jasen inquired with a disturbing frown.

Savana was silent for a while and did not know how to respond.

"No!" she said with a defensive denial of her guilt. "Why are you asking me this question?"

"You have been going out all the time and you conveniently leave our baby with Mama. You usually go for three to four hours,"

Jasen said. "If you are having an affair with someone, I am going to keep Jerry and I am going to ask you to leave," said Jasen.

Savana started to cry.

"I don't want to leave Jerry," cried Savana.

"You are an unfit mother. You leave your baby with Mama all the time and you lied to her all the time. How dare you tell her that you have a doctor's appointment all the time -did you forget that I am a doctor too? Are you sleeping with the doctor down the street?" asked Jasen.

Savana began to sob uncontrollably.

"I am going to get full custody of Jerry. We can settle it now and avoid going to court," Jasen suggested.

Savana agreed. Jerry was three now and he was growing fast into a handsome boy. Savana liked the idea of Jasen caring for Jerry and she knew he was not going to marry her. But Jasen loved her and she knew that too. She could not talk to him right now. He was extremely upset. She would talk to him when he felt better. Jasen felt deeply conflicted. He was angry at Savana's betrayal but he did not want to let her go. After all, she was the mother of his child and he loved her very much.

That night Jasen could not go to sleep and he got up in the middle of the night to check on Jerry.

He went to Jerry's room and found him deep asleep. Jasen was happy to see his son sleeping. He sat down for a while and just watched him sleeping. He cried and tear drops fell from his cheeks. "I am the luckiest man in the world to have a beautiful son and a beautiful Savana -the mother of my baby," Jasen said to himself. Finally, he saw Savana come in to check on Jerry and to her surprise, she saw Jasen sitting there. She hugged Jasen and started crying. "Oh, Jasen, I love you very much and I am sorry that I cheated on you and I promise you that I will not do it again. I want you to take care of Jerry because that is best for him.

I do not know what you are going to do with me," cried Savana in deep distress.

"I was going to ask you to leave, Savana, and I would take care of Jerry. As a matter of fact, I had my attorney file the custody papers in court," said Jasen sorrowfully.

Savana was too young to understand all of this. She cried and apologized to Jasen. Jasen was in love with her and that was all that mattered to Savana.

"I am going to give you another chance Savana, and I want you to take good care of Jerry."

Today I heard him say "daddy" for the first time and I was thrilled when I heard him. Do you ever just look at Jerry and see how beautiful he is?" Jasen asked.

Savana just cried and did not say anything.

The next day Jasen felt a little better. He realized how repentant Savana was and he wanted to forgive her.

Karolina was preparing dinner, when Savana, after shopping for toddler toys, dared to enter the kitchen for a tell all conversation with her mother-in-law.

"Hi Savana! How are you?" she asked. "I am okay. Jasen talked to me about Jerry. He asked me if I was having an affair with someone. I lied to him and he got very upset. I had to tell him the whole truth. He was going to ask me to leave and he was going to take custody of Jerry. He told me that he already had his attorney file custody for Jerry. I started to cry and cry. I apologized to him and promised that I was not going to do it again. He gave me another chance to stay and take care of Jerry," she explained to Karolina. Karolina did not respond.

"Let's prepare the dinner; Jasen Is hungry," Karolina curtly replied.

Little Jerry ran into to the kitchen and Savana was surprised to see him.

"Look who is here! "My little man!" She lifted him up and kissed him. "Are you hungry too?" she asked Jerry.

Jasen showed up and when he saw Jerry, he took him away from his mother.

"What is Jerry going to eat?" asked Jasen.

In an unspoken battle with Savana for dominance in her kitchen, Karolina answered, "I have his food ready: some fish and vegetables and mashed potatoes."

Chapter Ten

Jasen had been thinking about Savana a lot lately. He was struggling whether to marry her or not. Every day the more he saw Savana with his son Jerry, the more he wanted her. Jasen called his attorney and cancelled all the custody proceedings.

"What happened?" asked the attorney.

"I had a long conversation with Savana about what I was going to do with her," said Jasen. "Savana is too young to understand all these things. She does not have any money and she gave up her apartment, and it feels like I am taking care of two little kids." The attorney laughed.

"It just too big for her to understand and I love her very much. I am thinking of taking her with us to live in Italy," Jasen continued. "If I take her to Italy, she can learn many new things and then she can mature at the same time," Jasen confided in a patronizing voice. "I want you to meet Savana- she is beautiful and young and you should come and meet little Jerry," said Jasen to his cousin in his upscale law office.

"I will stop by and drop those papers to you. How is aunty Karolina?" asked the attorney.

"She is really doing well. She cares for Savana and loves her grandson. My mother has a lot of secrets but you already know that," said Jasen with a wink.

Karolina and Savana continued packing all their things ready to be shipped to Italy. They had only a few months before they left. Jasen wanted to talk to both them in the evening after dinner. They had ten boxes of stuff that needed to be shipped to his uncle in Italy. Jasen had a meeting with Karolina and Savana. The reason he wanted to meet with his mother was so she could understand why they were going with Savana to Italy.

"Yes, I want Savana to come with us for Jerry's sake. I want her to learn the Italian culture. She is young and pretty," said Karolina.

"I am not going to marry you, Savana," said Jasen. We will talk about it later but we have a lot of work to do. We have to get your passport and one for my beautiful son! He is going to have his first passport," sobbed Jasen. He was very emotional, crying and happy about his son Jerry. Savana was crying and happy and thanked Jasen for his forgiveness and for all he was doing on her behalf.

The next day, Karolina went to the Post Office where they were going to apply for both Savana and Jerry's passport. The passport clerk told them they would receive their passports in two weeks.

Savana was happy to hear that. They had two months to go before they left for Italy. They had packed most of their belongings and they sold all the furniture. Someone already bought the beds and dressers. They would come to get them before they left. Jasen told Savana not to buy too many clothes for Jerry and herself. We are going to shop for clothes when we get to Italy. Jasen heard from the realtor Italy, that the house had closed from escrow and now he was the new owner. He called his uncle right away to give him the good news. "I bought the house Uncle Angelo!"

"Congratulation! I am going to check it out right away. I am going to have some people to clean the house," said Angelo.

Jasen thanked his uncle and said good bye. Karolina appeared asking, "What's going on?"

"Oh Mama! I bought the house in Italy."

"Really?" Karolina asked in disbelief of her own good fortune in clinging to her Jasen.

"Yes, the realtor called me today. I called Uncle Angelo and told him the good news. Hs happy to hear that you would have a place to live as you age and he is going to have some people to start cleaning the house tomorrow," said Jasen.

Jasen was relieved they didn't have to go and look for a house when they got there. He knew his hands would be full with his new winery business. Jerry was beginning to be a big boy. He was talking and starting to make sense. Jasen was very proud of his son and he wanted to provide a stable home for his son and his schooling. Jasen's love for Savana was growing stronger and stronger and he desperately wanted to make love to her again and tell her his true feelings towards her. He could not wait anymore.

"Oh, Savana! I can't hold my feeling towards you. I love you Savana. You gave me a son and it is a blessing. I want to make love to you tonight," Jasen said panting and pouring out his heart.

Savana quickly agreed with a yearning sigh and replied with an intimate whisper: "We have not made love for such a long time now, my precious Jasen. I thought you had met an Italian woman to satisfy your desires."

"No, I bought vineyard and I know I will make money from it to support you and Jerry and my mother. Plus, Italy is a beautiful country and the Mediterranean weather is very good for you," said Jasen.

They didn't have to hide their making love to Karolina anymore. They went to Jasen's bedroom and made passionate unrestrained love. They missed each other and they made love for a very long time. They had one more month before they left for Italy.

Savana was very happy and excited about moving to Italy. Jerry was five years old now and he was really talkative. Jasen was thinking to teach Jerry how to speak Italian. He was planning to find him a tutor when they got there. July arrived and they gathered all their luggage and passports and off they went to the airport for their flight to Italy. Savana was very happy and Karolina was glad to see Savana smiling and very happy. The long flight to Italy took nine hours. They arrived at the airport, and they saw that his uncle Angelo and his Aunty Maria were waiting for them. They were very happy to meet Savana and little Jerry. They got in the car, and they drove them to their awe-inspiring villa. Toney had dinner and being exhausted from traveling- went to bed. In the morning, Maria prepared breakfast for them. Jasen told his uncle to take Savana and Jerry to go and see their new house. Karolina wanted to come too. It was a five-bedroom house overlooking the Mediterranean Sea. Savana loved the warm weather and the warm breeze. The house was beautiful and his Uncle Angelo and Aunty Maria had fixed up their house for them. Savana noticed all their things had arrived and Jasen had asked his uncle to buy all their furniture including all the kitchen items. On the following week, Jasen, Savana and Jerry moved into their new home and Karolina moved in two days later. Karolina fell in love with the house and especially the airy open kitchen completes with copper pans and windows that opened to an olive tree grove. On the large marble island stood various bottles of delicious estate cured olive oil. She was thinking of teaching Savana how to cook Italian foods. Maria, her sister-in-law, stopped to see them.

"My what a good-looking family!" Maria gushed kissing Savana on both cheeks in the Italian way of greeting. "Savana you look very pretty and young and you have a wonderful son," she said.

Savana thanked Maria.

"Would you like to go shopping with me tomorrow?" Maria asked.

"Yes" Savana replied. "Karolina is coming with us too."

Savana was very excited about the shopping trip. She planned what she was going to buy and asked Jasen to give her some money.

Jasen gave Savana one thousand euros'. Savana looked confused at the unfamiliar paper money. "I will teach you later," said Jasen.

"Meanwhile, have fun spending it!"

Maria arrived exactly at nine o'clock the next day. Savana and Karolina both walked out the door to greet her. They were all happy to see each other. Maria took them to these beautiful boutique stores. In one store, they observed a craftsman tool the leather he had stretched out to dry before them and then were amazed watching him definitely seen his genuine leather smelling satchels and designer purses. They purchased several hand-hewn leather items from this local artisan. Savana really enjoyed the trip and especially the oceanside. They sat down and sipped cappuccino in this intimate coffee shop and enjoyed strong Italian roast coffee, Italian coffee cake, and freshly sliced fruit in tall glass cups with hand whipped cream on top. They reveled together as they watched out the window the beautiful waves and the people swimming in the ocean. Savana stood up and walked out the mosaic decorated door towards the beach. She stood there and she saw an island not very far from where they were. She was excited and walked over quickly and asked Maria about the Island.

"Oh! I am glad you asked, Savana. That's Sicily," she said.

"It's part of Italy," said Karolina. "One day we are going to go there. They have a beautiful vineyard there. My father was going to buy a vineyard in Sicily but he changed his mind. They have many secrets there," she told Savana."

What kind of secrets?" Savana asked.

"I cannot share it with you right now. We will talk about it tonight," Karolina said.

Savana enjoyed their day excursion into a completely different culture. The experience seemed to harmonize with what she felt ringing in her soul and her DNA. At the same time, she discovered that Italy was definitely very different from America. The pace was very slow there and they took time to express their emotions to one another often with dramatic arm gestures.

They were all tired when they got home. Karolina told her Maria that they would see them around seven for dinner. Jasen and little Jerry just got home in time as well to see Savana and Karolina. Jerry was happy to see his mother and grandmother. Savana gave him a very big hug.

"I missed you, Jerry!" his mother told him. "I missed you too mama," he replied looking mature in his pristine school uniform. Jerry was attending a private Catholic school where they taught Italian and English and Jerry now was fluent in both languages.

"We are going over to Angelo and Maria's villa for dinner," said Karolina.

'How come?" asked Jasen.

"Savana made a discovery today," said Karolina.

"What was it?" asked Jasen.

"She discovered Sicily!" replied Karolina.

Chapter
Eleven

Jasen gave a big laugh and said "I am glad Savana saw the island of Sicily because we are going to take a trip there next week. I want to buy a vineyard," said Jasen. "I want Angelo and Maria to tell you and Savana all the secrets about Sicily," said Jasen. They all had a traditional Italian dinner pasta, steak, and salad with gelato for dessert. "Savana wanted to know the secrets about Sicily?" asked Angelo.

"Yes, I am very curious," said Savana.

"We all are going to take a trip there next week. I am thinking of buying a vineyard. I know, Grandpa wanted to buy a vineyard there but changed his mind," said Jasen. "Why did he change his mind Uncle Angelo?" asked Jasen.

"There were so many different people to go through before he could make a deal and many secret deals, but they were careful they did not get caught.

"Before Sicily became an island, it was a kingdom. The history of Sicily was very important. Things have changed- now much of Sicily is commercialized. I want to take a trip over there next week and check the vineyards out and then I will decide to buy one or not. I have seen some of the vineyards are for sale and I want all of us to go," said Jasen.

"We have to fly from Florence to Palermo, which is must easier and much shorter than taking the ferry," said his uncle "and it only takes an hour and twenty-five minutes to fly.

"I want to go some other time because of Jerry. It will be too much for him," said Savana.

Jasen agreed. "I will just take my uncle with me."

"It is a good idea for both of you to go and leave us here. You go and check it out. If it is okay then we'll go and visit," said Karolina.

They all said good night to one another and they went back home under the sparkling black velvet sky. "There is more work to be done here. The winery needs new equipment. We need to renovate the restaurant into an intimate enchanting cozy cafe. I will let Savana take care of that," said Jasen.

"I love to design interiors and it will give me something to do. "I want to start tomorrow," said Savana.

"We need to hire more workers too," said Savana.

Later that week they took the first flight to Sicily. They flew from Florence to Palermo which is the capital of Sicily. They arrived at noon and hired a rental car to drive them to the hotel. Jasen found Sicily to be a very beautiful island and the people were very friendly. He knew that Sicily was mixed with other races that Jasen did not know about.

Jasen felt very strange when they arrived in Sicily. He felt like he was in a new country. It did not feel like Italy at all. He also noticed that the people had darker skin and spoke with a different accent than the normal Italian. He wanted to ask his uncle why, but he decided to ask him later.

When they got up the next day, they went to meet Bruno who was selling the vineyard. Bruno was happy to meet them and he gave them a tour of the vineyard and Jasen was very impressed.

They talked about the prices and everything that comes with the vineyard. Jasen noticed that it needed some work with the restaurant and the wine tasting area. Jasen told Bruno that he would get back to him on the next day.

"Where are you from?" asked Bruno.

"Jasen, my nephew is from America and he has moved here to buy a vineyard," replied Angelo.

"Very good. Sicily is a beautiful island and the food is very good here and you meet different people from all over the world," said Bruno.

"Yes, I see that," replied Jasen. They said good bye and they went back to their hotel. Jasen asked his uncle why some Sicilian people are darker than the others. His uncle explained to Jasen that Sicily was racially mixed and at one point they believed they were mixed with Arab, German, French, Spanish, and English. If you taste their food too it is very different from regular Italian foods. Their food is spicier because of the different cultures.

"Let me ask you Uncle Angelo, did you like the vineyard we saw today?" asked Jasen.

"Your grandfather was going to buy a vineyard from here but then he changed his mind," said Angelo.

"Why did grandpa change his mind?" asked Jasen.

"Your grandmother, who was the cousin of the King of Italy, obviously did not like the island and the people that lived here. You see back in those days; this island was very different. It was very difficult to move around. It was very primitive.

It took days to come from Italy to get to this island. Your grandmother was very scared of the sea and also the food," said his uncle.

"Were those the only reasons?" asked Jasen.

"No," said his uncle. "We will talk about this later." Jasen could not sleep that night. He had to make up his mind by tomorrow. He thought about what his uncle told him.

"There must be a reason why his grandfather did not buy the vineyard from here," he said to himself. The next day, Jasen took a walk down to the seaside. It was crammed full of people just having coffee and enjoying the beautiful Sicilian Mediterranean weather. He bought a cup of coffee and sat on the chair at his table which faced the clear blue ocean in a cozy little cove and he watched the rhythmic high tide waves crashing onto the shore. The gulls were cawing and competing for the food that had washed upon the shore at high tide.

He thought about Savana and little Jerry. He thought about Jerry's future and he made up his mind that Sicily was not the place for Jerry. He is better off in Italy and America. Angelo followed him down to the seaside and he asked Jasen if he had made up his mind.

"Yes, I have made up my mind. I am not going to buy I." "Why?" his uncle asked. "I have been thinking about Jerry. He is growing up to be a very smart boy and very soon he is going to high school and then to college. I am thinking about his future and I can see that Sicily is not a place for him.

"We are going to be travelling back and forth. It is going to be too much," said Jasen.

"I am glad you thought about that. Sicily is a kind of place to come and enjoy the food and the Mediterranean weather," said his uncle.

"Let's go and see Bruno," said Jasen. Bruno was waiting for them. "What have you decided Jasen?" Bruno asked.

"I have made up my mind. I could not go to sleep last night. I kept tossing and turning and this morning, I got up and walked down to the seaside and what a beautiful sight. I wished I was young again but now I have a beautiful son and he is growing up very quickly and I have to take care of his schooling," explained Jasen. "I am not going to take the offer," said Jasen.

"I remember the story of your uncle when I found out your last name. I knew it right away about your grandfather." Bruno turned to Angelo, and said: "Your father was very wealthy and he came here and tried to buy a vineyard just like your nephew and I did not want to tell you that this was the same vineyard that your father wanted to buy. He came here with your mother. You and your sister were not with them."

"My father Bruno senior, met them and they wanted to purchase the vineyard" he said. "Now here is his grandson who is trying to do the same thing!" They all burst out laughing." Probably there is a curse on this vineyard and they started to laugh again.

"How old is this vineyard?" Jasen asked " About 80 years old," Bruno replied.

"That's about right when I was born round about that time when my parents came here," said Angelo.

"What a small world," said Jasen.

"I remembered my dad told me that you have a beautiful sister," said Bruno.

"My sister's name is Karolina and she is Jasen's mother," said Angelo. "I remember, my dad used to tell me the story that your father used to invite them to come and visit his vineyard in Tuscany. He would show them all his vineyards and they used to dine at his restaurant and afterwards they went down to the ocean and walked on the beach.

Your parents were wonderful people and very wealthy as well. "Are you taking over all the vineyards now?" Bruno asked. " Yes, I am" replied Angelo. "Jasen bought the Ferrari's vineyard after the Ferrari family moved to Switzerland."

"We have a lot of work to do in that vineyard," said Jasen.

"That is what happens when you buy a vineyard. You have to repair a lot of things and you have to spend a lot of money if you want to have a successful vineyard," said Bruno. "My son Gabriele is not into vineyards but he is a very successful restaurant and bar owner. He has several restaurants in Sicily and several in Venice and three right there in Tuscany," Bruno proudly said.

Chapter Twelve

"How old is your son?" Jasen asked.

"My son is 45 years old and he is not married. He is looking for a wife now," he said.

Are you married Jasen?" Bruno asked. "No, I am not married but I brought the mother of my son with me but I am not planning to marry her any time soon," said Jasen.

"Why is that?' Bruno asked "I am too busy," said Jasen.

"What did you do in America?" asked Bruno. "I used to be a surgeon," replied Jasen.

"Can you still practice medicine here?" asked Bruno.

"No, I am a cardiologist and I will probably have a clinic later on. Italy has a very low heart problem compared to America. It has to do with the climate and foods," said Jasen.

I want you to meet my son Gabriele Messina. He will be coming to Tuscany to his restaurant next week. We can go and have lunch at his restaurant near the ocean and meet him," said Bruno. The next week, they went and met Gabriele and he was happy to meet them. He asked them to come to see his new restaurant in Tuscany.

"How many restaurants do you have and how many bars?" asked Jasen.

I have thirty restaurant and one hundred bars."

"Wow, you must have a lot of money!" replied Jasen.

I am going to open one in London, New York, and Dubai in the summer," said Gabriele. "I am looking for a wife to help me."

"A good-looking guy like you, you should not have any problem at all. There are so many pretty women but good loving women are very hard to find!" sighed Jasen.

"I agree", said Gabriele.

"How about you, are you married?" Gabriele asked.

"No, I am not married but I live with the mother of my son but I don't think we are going to get married," said Jasen.

"Why is that?" asked Gabriele.

"Just too busy" was Jasen's curt reply.

"Bring your family to the restaurant; I want to meet all of them!" Gabriele said.

"I will do that," Jasen eagerly replied.

Many years passed and Jasen was always busy with his vineyard so time flew by in raising Jerry. Savana was a very good mother and Jerry was very close to his mother as is the Italian tradition.

When Jerry was finished with his high school and he was getting ready to go to college, Jasen had a long discussion with Savana concerning where Jerry should go to college. Savana suggested that he should go to college in Italy. It was close to them and he could also help in the vineyard and with the paper work.

But Jasen disagreed. "I want him to go to college in America because of the high standards in business and financial proceedings. I want him to be able to run this vineyard if something happens to you or me," said Jasen.

"We'll let him decide that," said Savana. Jerry was very excited to go to college.

"Have you decided what college you want to attend son?" Jasen asked him.

"Yes, I want to go to Harvard," he replied.

"You need to be more specific Jerry," Jasen said.

"Okay, dad, I want to study business!" he told his father. "I see all these vineyards and I was thinking who is going to take care of them if something happens to you or mom?" he questioned with mature foresight.

"I am very happy to hear that Jerry," said his father. Harvard started in the fall and he was going to live in the dormitory there. Savana prepared his beddings, towels and his dishes.

"I want to go shopping with you mom and I want to talk to you about dad," said Jerry. The next day Jerry and Savana went shopping in some nearby shops and Jerry was very happy to spend time with his mother. They had their lunch at Cafe Lola.

"Mom, are you and dad ever going to get married?" asked Jerry hopefully.

"I don't think your dad wants to get married. I wanted to get married when we were back in America. He was not sure even to bring me here to Italy and when they came back from their trip with Grandma, he made up his mind to take me to Italy with you and your grandmother but not to get married. Your grandmother, Karolina, wanted your dad to marry an Italian woman and I don't know if your dad is still thinking about marriage," said Savana.

"I am going to college now, and I love you mom and I feel bad for you. I know, that Karolina still feels that you are not good enough for my dad," Jerry opined.

"I am glad that you see that, Jerry. Sometimes, I think if I meet someone that will love me and take care of me, I will marry that man," said Savana with teary eyes. "I am going to be forty-two years old next week, and I feel like I am unwanted, and that I don't fit in this society. Often, I feel like I am an outcast or that I am a victim of discrimination," said Savana.

They both had tears in their eyes.

"Mom, I see everything and I notice how dad and Karolina have been treating you. I want you to find a job, mom, so you can be independent. I am glad that you got your driver's license. I know dad wants you to work in the vineyard helping the workers and that's good but I want you Mom to be financially independent so you do not need to rely on dad."

"I am doing that very slowly and I told your dad yesterday that I was going to look for a job and study the Italian language," Savana told Jerry.

When they arrived back at their villa, Karolina and Jasen greeted them. Over a glass of wine, Jerry's grandmother shared, "Both of your parents will be going with you when your school starts," said Karolina. "I want to come along too, if I feel better," said Karolina.

"What did you buy on this shopping trip with your mother, Jerry?" his father asked.

"I bought some clothes, some sweaters, four pair of shoes and jogging pants." I know, Harvard is in the States of Massachusetts and it is pretty cold there," said Jerry.

"Mom helped me buy sheets, towels, soaps and other necessities," said Jerry.

"I am glad that you went shopping with your mom and that gave you sometime to talk," said Jasen.

"Yes, that was very nice to go shopping with her and I was able to have a meaningful conversation with her."

"Next week is your mom's birthday and do you know how old she is going to be?" asked Jasen.

"Yes, I know mom's birthday- she is going to be forty-two".

"Where are we going to take her for her birthday?" asked Jerry.

"I am thinking of taking her to Messina - a Sicilian restaurant. Uncle Angelo and Aunt Maria are going to be joining us as well," said Jasen. Jerry informed his dad: "I am going to wait and buy my computer when we get to America. I want to get an apple computer and iPad as well. I have to get an iPhone to use over there to call you and mom."

"We will be going with you to Harvard," said Jasen.

"Grandma already told me that she might come with us too," said Jerry. "She has not been to New England. She refused to come with dad because it was too cold."

She did not like the New England states," Jasen said. "Did she come to your graduation?" asked Jerry. "She came to my graduation because she was very happy that I was going to medical school," said Jasen.

You have to study hard and work hard to be successful. I am glad that you've chosen Harvard. It is one of the best schools in the world and I am glad that you chose to go to Harvard business school. A business degree will be very helpful with our wine business," said Jasen. His father thanked him and Jasen was very proud of his Jerry. He reminded Jasen of his late father. He was a very good business man and that was why their vineyard was very successful and made a lot of money. Let's go and check what mom and grandmother are doing," said his father.

"Shall we eat now?" asked Savana. I am ravished with hunger!".

They all sat around the table and enjoyed their salad, fish and antipasti. "I am very proud of you Jerry! You are just like your father; you are also going to Harvard and your grandfather would be very proud of you if he was still alive," said Karolina.

"Are you going with us grandma?" asked Jerry.

"Yes, I've made up my mind. I am very happy you are going to Harvard," said Karolina.

Tuesday was Savana's birthday. She was very excited. Jasen bought her an ocean blue dress and Jasen asked Savana to wear the dress that he bought her.

Chapter Thirteen

Savana looked very pretty and happy. They all rode in the car and left for the restaurant. The restaurant was beautiful and Gabriele was expecting them. He came and greeted them at the door. He took a look at Savana; he knew right away this was the girl that his dad and Jasen were talking about. He led them to their table and Jasen introduced Savana, Karolina, Maria and he had already met Angelo. "The dinner will be on the house," said Gabriele. The restaurant was packed with people and Savana recognized some Americans. The food was very good which is why people kept going there. They ate fish, pasta, salad, steaks and desserts. Gabriele brought Savana a huge birthday cake made from fruits, rum, and almond nuts. He also served his special homemade pistachio gelato. They sang Happy Birthday to Savana and Gabriele offered Savana ten free dinners that she could use the next time she wanted to come to the restaurant.

Savana was very happy and Jerry was very happy and the entire restaurant stood up and honored her as she left. Gabriele kept looking at Savana. Savana looked back and waved at him. Gabriele called his father right away, "I met her; she is beautiful!" I see the problem they soon will be facing.". Their son is ready to attend school in Harvard in America. Savana will be really lonely in Italy," said Gabriele. "She is going to travel with Jasen and Jerry to Harvard. He is a handsome boy. He looks like his mother."

"Did you talk to her tonight at all?" asked her father.

"No, but she waved at me when they were leaving," said Gabriele. I will see her again. She is going to come here. This is the girl I have been waiting for and fate has brought us together," said Gabriele.

"If it's meant to be, she will show up here. They are very nice people as well as very wealthy. They don't want to send Jerry to go to college here in Italy instead, they are sending him to Harvard. Jasen too, went to school at Harvard medical school," Bruno said. He is going to help his father with the vineyard business when he graduates. He does not want to be a doctor like his father or an attorney like his father's cousin." said Bruno.

"Smart young boy. He loves his mother," said Gabriele "I wish I could help Jerry and Savana. I can just feel her pain. I felt she wants to get married to Jasen. I felt that Jasen wants to marry her," said Gabriele He told me that when they came over to Sicily- when they came and looked at the vineyard."

"It was a coincidence that he came to see the same vineyard that his grandfather wanted to buy," said Bruno.

"Very interesting, God has answered my prayer," he told his father.

"We all know, that fate is a powerful thing. I have been looking for a wife for a very long time. I looked everywhere and here is my wife," said Gabriele. "They are leaving this weekend to take Jerry to Harvard. They will be gone for one week to see he gets all settled down. When they return, Savana is going to be looking for a job. "

"She can come and work here!" Gabriele said hopefully and gallantly. "But she will probably go and work in Jasen's vineyard.

I overhead the restaurant in the vineyard needs fixing," said Bruno. I am having lunch with Angelo tomorrow and I will bring it up to him about Savana working at your restaurant. Jasen listens to him all the time," said Bruno.

"I am going to Sicily tomorrow and I will be back on Friday. On Saturday morning, I am flying to New York" said Gabriel. I am going to buy her a ring and I am going to give it to her when I take her to Sicily," said Gabriele.

His father laughed really loud. "I am glad that you are dreaming son," said Bruno.

"Father, Savana really looked beautiful in Mediterranean blue," crooned his son.

"Well, I'll leave cupid to do his thing. I am going to bed now." and Bruno said good night to his son. Gabriele closed the restaurant and went home. He could not go to sleep that night as he was thinking about Savana.

On the other side of town, Savana was also thinking about Gabriele. She did not have his phone number but she remembered the name of the restaurant and she was going to call him in the morning. Savana slept late that morning and to her surprise, her son Jerry woke her up and when she was awake announced, "Mom, I asked Dad if I could take you for breakfast at the Sicilian restaurant where we ate last night. I will drive there. They are open for breakfast at nine o'clock," said Jerry. "What time is it now?" asked Savana.

"It's eight o'clock," said Jerry.

Savana got up took her shower and got dressed and off they went to the restaurant. Gabriele was very surprised to see them. "Jerry wants to bring me here for breakfast!" Savana said with a twinkle in her eye.

"That's a great surprise," said Gabriele. "Jerry, I heard you're going to Harvard?"

"I am and I am looking forward to it but I am going to miss my mom. I told her to come and visit me," Jerry lamented.

"Don't worry, she will come and visit you," said Gabriele. The waitress brought Italian pastries, scrambled eggs, orange juice, and toast. Gabriele was able to talk to Savana. "Do you want to work Savana while Jerry studies at Harvard?" Gabriele asked.

"Yes, do you have any job openings?" she asked hopefully.

"Yes, I have all kinds of work," he said. You can be in charge of the kitchen and the staff as well," offered Gabriele ."I would love to say 'yes, I'll start tomorrow' to your kind offer, but we are taking Jerry to Harvard Business school and we will be gone for one week. As soon as we come back, I will come and start to work with you," Savana replied joyfully. Jerry was very thankful to Gabriele and very happy for his mother. They said goodbye to Gabriele and he gave Savana his phone number and asked her to call him if she needed any help. Savana thanked him and they said good bye and went home.

Savana thought about Gabriele and how very thankful she was that he gave her the biggest opportunity. She could now take care of herself and she could go and see Jerry whenever she wanted. She was missing her only son already.

"Mom stop crying! I will text you every day to see how you are doing at the restaurant. Gabriele likes you and I know he will take care of you."

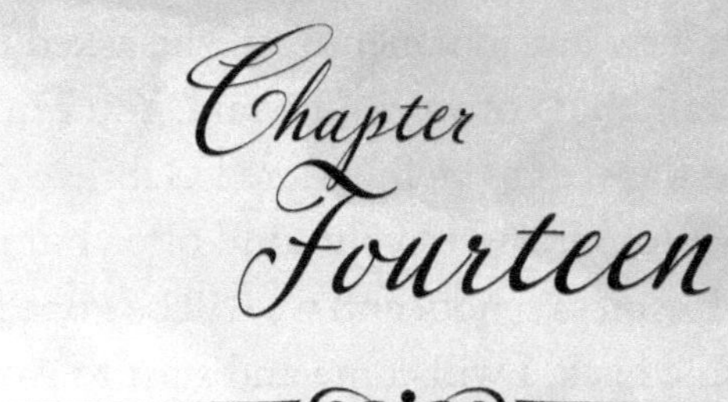

Chapter Fourteen

"Let's go home, dad probably is looking for us," Jerry said.

Jasen was waiting for them in the kitchen when they got home. "There you are," I was waiting for both of you. Did you have a nice breakfast?" asked Jasen.

"Yes, it was more than nice," Savana replied and excused herself to freshen up in her room.

"Yes" replied Jerry, I think my prayers for Mom were answered. Gabriele gave mom a job in the restaurant," said Jerry.

"Oh! Really!" Jasen said surprised and a bit suspicious of Gabriele's motives. Jasen had noticed how Gabriele could not take his eyes off Savana at dinner. How did your mom feel?"

"Mom was very happy and thanked Gabriele. She is going to start when you both come back from Harvard," said Jerry.

"I see that Karolina pretty much controls the family, not dad," complained Jerry. She never wanted you Dad to marry mom. Just then Karolina requested Jasen's presence in his study. Savana joined her son in the kitchen conversation.

"I am glad that I am going to school, Mom, I want to be something in this world. I want to make the world to be a better place," Jerry said with a kind and idealistic voice. "I want you to come and see me mom and I don't want you to wait for dad! Please don't waste your time and beauty waiting for Dad to ask you to marry him," Jerry pleaded.

"I want to get married and have a family. I am getting too old to be married," complained Savana.

"You are not old mother. I see men looking at you. I think Gabriele likes you mom," Jerry lovingly confided.

"Oh! Jerry, he must have many girlfriends," said Savana.

"Mom, I won't be very surprised if he falls in love with you and I don't mind at all, mom." He looks like a nice guy who is financially stable," Jerry said.

"I want you to study hard Jerry. Harvard business school is one of the best in the world. You will probably have your own business one day," Savana said proudly.

The next day Jerry and Savana returned home late in the afternoon. Jasen and Karolina were not home but they left a note. They went shopping and they would be home very shortly.

"Wow! Mom, they went shopping," said Jerry. "They are always going shopping together."

"She tells him what to buy all the time," laughed Savana with a sarcastic tone. "Here they come," said Savana. "Did you both have a nice time?"

"Guess what! We went to buy more clothes for Jerry," said Jasen. Let's go and eat." We must rise early tomorrow morning," said Savana. They all boarded the first flight to Boston. Jerry was happy to see both of his parents traveling with him and his favorite grandmother, Karolina. During the flight his grandmother spoke encouraging words to her only grandson:

"I am very proud of you Jerry; you are just like your father; you both will graduate from Harvard. You are smart like your father and I know you are going to do very well!"

They arrived in Boston on Tuesday afternoon. It was spring time in New England and the cherry blossoms were in full bloom. They checked into their hotel, ordered clam chowder and lobster bisque to enjoy in room dining and to get some rest because of the time differences. They all went to bed early that night. Savana could not go to sleep thinking of Jerry. She was not going to see her son until Christmas time. She already was planning to take a trip to go and see Jerry in the summer.

"You can come to Italy in the summer if you want Jerry," said his father.

"I need a job dad, I just can 't come and do nothing," answered Jerry.

"Wow! you sound like your dad when he was going to school," Karolina proudly responded.

"I know dad doesn't want me to just be sitting around and hanging out," Jerry said with a confident maturity.

"If you want to work son, I will have a job for you, but if you want to hang around with your mom, it's okay too," said Jasen.

It was time to say good bye to Jerry. They cried but were very happy for him. His mom told him to study hard and to call her once in a while. They said goodbye and left Jerry with his classmates and school. Karolina was very happy to go with them to Harvard because the last time they were there was when Jasen first attended. She never had been back there until this time. Savana was all quiet and she cried a little. She missed her son and now she felt lonely and empty.

"When are you going to start working at the restaurant?" Jasen asked hoping to lift her spirit and focus her thoughts on the future.

"I will be starting next Tuesday," she replied despondently.

"What will you be doing there?" Karolina asked.

"I will be in charge of the kitchen and all the staff."

"Can you do all that Savana? Sounds like a very big responsibility," said Karolina.

"I am glad I am doing this; I will be making my own money to be able to go and visit Jerry sometimes. "I don't think Jasen needs me at the vineyard. He just hired four hundred workers and he is going to hire four hundred more," Savana responded in her defense.

"I am still going to need you there to help for the decorations and customer service, but if you want to make your own money, it's okay too," said Jasen kindly, knowing that his mother had just underestimated Savana's abilities on purpose.

"I will come and help when I have some free times," said Savana.

They all flew back home and Jasen started his first day at the vineyard. He had to remind himself that he was no longer a doctor but a Vintner. He had to remember that all the time. It was hard for him to adapt himself. He was going to be stomping grapes all his life.

He met all his 400 employees-young and old- He wanted us to meet all his financial employees. These are going to be the most important people who will be in charge of running the business. The second group of people are the people who are going to be planting the grapes. He decided to hire 500 more people to plant grapes. The next group of people were the people who were going to harvest the grapes and who were actually going to make wine in the winery. It looked like a lot of work for Jasen, but he was going to bring his uncle Angelo tomorrow to help him set up the winery. He bought all new machinery to process the wine and to bottle it to be ready to distribute this wine around the world. His brand and the winery would be called *Paradiso* after the famous Italian poet Dante and his Chianti would be made from his Sangiovese red wine varietal grapes. Jasen named this top-of-the-line wine *Angelo* in honor of his uncle and the angels!

On Tuesday, Savana would begin her first day of work helping Gabriele in his restaurant. She started at nine o'clock in the morning and got off at five p.m. Deep down inside, Jasen wanted Savana to work with him in the vineyard. But he didn't want to marry her so he decided to leave it at that. Jasen had this strong feeling that Gabriel was going to fall in love with Savana. She was relatively young and still very beautiful. His mother Karolina made a comment to him two weeks ago during her birthday dinner. She saw Gabriele give a very long stare at Savana. The kind of look that you are falling in love with someone. "Karolina asked Jasen, "Whose idea was it for them to go and have breakfast at Gabriele's restaurant?"

"It was Jerry's idea," said Jasen. "Jerry asked me if I was going to marry his mother and I said no. I saw the sadness in his eyes."

"You better find yourself an Italian woman to marry really fast. I don't think Jerry likes what he is seeing between you and Savana. He is a very smart boy," warned Karolina.

Finally, it was Tuesday morning and Savana was very excited about her new job. She took a shower and got dressed and hopped inside her old model Fiat and drove to work. Gabriele was already waiting for her. "Welcome Savana!" said Gabriele. "You look beautiful this morning," I want to introduce you to everyone you are going to be working with. There are going to be forty people and most of them have been working here for a very long time. They will also be teaching you how things are done around here." Savana tried to learn every expectation in the work culture of the restaurant, and she took copious notes as well. She wrote every employee's name and then learned how to pronounce them. Everything was foreign to her and the only language she knew was the English language. She was very determined to study the Italian language and accounting. The first few weeks were rough for her, but she finally learned how everything worked.

One day, Gabriele asked her to stop by after work. He noticed that she looked unhappy all the time. He asked her to have dinner with him and she agreed. "Are you happy here Savana?" he asked her.

"Very much so," she replied.

"Is everything alright with you?" he asked.

"No, I miss my son a lot and I am not happy at home. I am looking for a place to stay. I want my son to come and stay with me when he comes home this summer," she said.

"Don't worry, I already found a house for you and you can move in anytime you want," generously offered Gabriele. She looked astonished and surprised. "You what! You found a place for me! "She turned to Gabriele and thanked him with tears coming down from her eyes.

"I overheard you and little Jerry talking about it the last time you were here. I saw the sadness in your eyes. I decided to find you a house where you and Jerry can stay. I know Jasen won't marry you. His mother wants an Italian woman for him. It was pretty obvious when I saw them at your birthday dinner," Gabriele explained. Savana agreed to everything he said.

"Karolina brings many problems to us and Jasen listens to her all the time," Savana said in a mournful tone.

Italian mothers are very controlling when it comes to the women their sons want to marry," explained Gabriele. "You see, Jasen's family is very wealthy with "old" money. This wealth entitlement goes back to his great, great grandfather. His mother, Karolina is very wealthy as well. These kinds of people always want to marry their own kind," explained Gabriele. "I am not Italian- I am a Sicilian. We are all about love! And eat and be merry!" he said with a light laugh that warmed her heart. "Have you been observing them the way they eat, the way they talk and the way they dress? We talk a little differently from the classical Italian. We pronounce our words differently from them."

"When would you like to move into your new home?" Gabriele asked.

"This weekend" she replied.

Savana was very excited about her new house. She called Jerry right away.

"Hi Mom! How's your new job?" he asked.

"Very good. I am going to school in the evening taking the Italian language and accounting.

"I am very proud of you Mom," said Jerry.

"I have better exciting news to tell you. Gabriele found me a house and I am moving in this weekend. I don't have very much, Jerry, but I am glad I am out from that monster's home," said Savana.

"Have you told dad? Jerry asked with some trepidation.

"No, not yet," said Savana. "I will talk to you tomorrow."

Savana finally arrived home. Karolina and Jasen already had dinner.

"Are you going to have something to eat Savana?" Karolina asked.

"I already ate" replied Savana. "I need to talk to you Jasen," said Savana. "Gabriele found me a house and it's a beautiful house. I have decided to move in this weekend. I already told Jerry about it. I don't have very much but a least I have a place to stay," said Savana gratefully.

"I am glad that you are getting things on your own and you are in good hands. We have known his family for a very long time. His grandfather and his great grandfather were very rich. I am glad he's helping you out," said Jasen.

"I am taking Italian and accounting in the nearby college. I found out how important it is to know how to speak Italian because most of them don't know how to speak English. It is really hard working in the restaurant. Everything is in Italian. I suggested to Gabriele to have Italian and English labels on the items we use mostly.

He said that during the summer we have a lot of tourists from America and Europe who come and eat at the restaurant."

"I am glad you are working there and you will be a great help to Gabriele. He has restaurants all over Europe and America," Jasen said.

"Wow! Your family and his have known each other for a long time. That is very interesting," said Savana.

She excused herself to go to bed. Karolina walked into Jasen's room. "I heard all your conversations and I am very impressed about Savana. Gabriele is going to fall in love with her and probably will marry her. He found her a house and I wonder what else he's going to give her?" asked Karolina sarcastically.

"Oh, Mom! Stop making fun of Savana! You know you caused all these things. You said that she's not good enough for me. Guess what! She is going to school taking the Italian language and accounting," said Jasen. "I still love Savana but we cannot all live together under one roof," said Jasen. "Come on Jasen, get it over with, start looking for an Italian wife. There are many good ones around. Your uncle Angelo will find you one," said Karolina. "I am going to keep a watch on Savana," said Karolina.

"Forget it mother, leave her alone and let her enjoy her life," Jasen pleaded.

Savana did not have much to pack. She did not have any furniture or anything for the kitchen. Gabriele told Savana not to worry. He would completely furnish the house from elegant draperies to practical kitchen appliances.

Savana packed her meager belongings and quickly left the house. Jasen had already left for the vineyard and Karolina was cooking in the kitchen. "Leaving Savana?" asked Karolina.

Karolina was really surprised to see her leaving. "I am cooking all this food Savana for you and Jasen," said Karolina.

"No thanks, I am not hungry and I better go now," she said. She formally said good bye to Karolina and left. Her car was filled up with the only belonging she owned.

Chapter
Sixteen

—⚜—

Her new house was on an olive tree covered hill overlooking the beautiful Mediterranean ocean.

She loved the view and the cool breeze.

The next morning, she decided to go shopping. As she was getting ready to leave, her phone rang. It was Gabriele. "Good morning, dear Savana! How are you this morning?" he asked.

His voice felt like the bright sun outside shining warmly inside her soul.

"I am good Gabriele. I am just getting ready to go shopping."

"Well, I have already purchased the curtains as a gift for you, my sweet Savana. The curtain connoisseur would like to meet with you soon so that you can tell them the color and the style you desire. You need to make an appointment with them to come to your new home and measure the windows. I also selected the most expensive silk fabric. You can call them right now," Gabriele kindly suggested.

"Do you want to come over here and help me?" Savana asked Gabriele with a flirty voice. "We could always cuddle and kiss behind the curtain samples!" she offered with a new freedom resounding in her heart.

"Sure, when you put it in that context," Gabriele laughed, "I would love to come and help you."

After arriving and admiring Savana's little touches of design, he spoke with visible concern:

"But Savana, you don't even have a bed to sleep on!"

"Oh, it's fine, Gabriele", Savana replied with an audible moan of displeasure. "I can just sleep on the floor. I just want to leave that horrid house where I have been living with such disrespect!" Savanna cried with an uncharacteristic tone of anger and frustration. "I just don't want to be around Karolina any longer."

"I don't blame you," Gabriele said. "You can go and sleep in our hotel, or I also have the guest room where you can sleep," offered Gabriele.

"I appreciate the offer but I think this carpeted floor will be just fine," said Savana.

"Okay then, I better go and get us something to eat," said Gabriele.

Just as Gabriele left, Savana's son Jerry called her. "Hi mom, how are you?"

"Bon Journo my son! I am very happy to hear your voice. How are you?" and "How's school?" Savana asked with motherly concern.

"I am doing very well at school. Have you moved mom?" Jerry asked.

"Yes, I have moved. I don't have anything but my clothes. I just wanted to get away from your grandma. I will be sleeping on the floor tonight!" she said with a slight laugh. Actually, I am so blessed to have Gabriele as my knight in shiny armor. He is taking care of my every need with a kind of generosity I have never experienced before!"

Gabriele ordered all the furniture for me and today the curtain people came and measured all the windows.

"I am very happy to hear that mom," Jerry said with sincerity.

"You will love this house; it sits on the hill overlooking the Mediterranean Sea. It is just so beautiful!"

"Well mom, I have some good news for you too. My summer school break is next month," said Jerry with homesick excitement in his voice.

"That's soon son," said Savana.

"Yes, mom," said Jerry. "I hope dad remembers that," Jerry replied looking for reassurance. "He told me to come and work in the vineyard.

"I will call him to remind him," his mother kindly offered. Well son, Gabriele has arrived with our dinner. I must go now while he and the food are still hot!"

Jerry laughed at his mother's racy pun and said good bye.

"Who have you been talking to?" asked Gabriele.

"My son, Jerry," said Savana.

"Well let's have dinner before it gets too cold," Gabriele suggested with love shining from his gorgeous eyes. They didn't talk very much. Savana was very quiet and Gabriele just stared at her lost in his love thoughts.

"Karolina is getting ready to find a wife for Jasen," Savana said breaking the ice. She is going to cook this big dinner tomorrow night. He is going have an Italian woman over who he met when they were here eighteen years ago. She is working for his Uncle Angelo. Gabriele asked Savana if she already met the girl.

"No, I was back in America pregnant with Jerry. Actually, he met and dated two Italian women. One of them was an accountant at Angelo's vineyard and the other one a manager. Jasen liked the brunette Sophia better than the blond girl. But when they returned, he did not want either woman. He wanted to marry me as the mother of his only son. He said we should wait to get married until Jerry grew bigger. The next thing that he told me was that I should come with them to Italy only to be Jerry's caretaker. We started packing all our belongings and sold the house. Jerry was growing up quickly and began to say words in sentences and Jasen was very proud of him and happy.

But Karolina was the main problem here and her son Jasen listened to her all the time. "If I did not sleep with him, he would never get married and probably live with his mother forever," Savana said with disgust. Gabriele tried to explain Karolina's negative behavior. "You see Savana, Karolina does not really like you. That's the way Italian mothers are. They do not want their son to marry a woman who is poor. As far as Karolina is concerned, you are low class. You are not worthy to marry her son."

"My that is harsh compared to American values. My parents are hardworking lawyers with a good standing in the community. Are Sicilian mothers like that too?" asked Savana.

"No, we are not like the Italians at all. We are all about amore. Everything is all about love and warm affection."

"I would like to take you to dinner tomorrow night at our restaurant if you like, or we can go somewhere else," said Gabriele.

"Yes, we are just decorating the new house so we should go to your lovely restaurant and have dinner there. It has a beautiful view of the ocean," said Savana.

"The house should look beautiful tomorrow after my interior designers leave," said Gabriele.

"Yes, it should be beautiful!" replied Savana.

"I will pick you up at 7 pm tomorrow night," Gabriele said affectionately while wrapping her in his arms with an intimate hug. He left Savana alone in her new house. Gabriele was falling "head over heels" in love with Savana. He continually thought about her. She is such a beautiful woman. He felt compassion for her situation. He thought to himself that Jasen had really missed a beautiful woman who is the mother of their handsome son.

The next day he went to the restaurant to check what was on the menu for dinner with Savana. He checked all the reservations and he saw Jasen and his mother's name were on the list. Gabriele was a very handsome man and Savana was happy that, unlike with Jasen, they were close in age.

"I have a surprise to tell you Savana," said Gabriele.

"What is it?" she asked.

I stopped by at the restaurant before I came here. I checked how many people are coming to the restaurant tonight. I checked the reservation lists and guess who I saw on the lists?" said Gabriele.

"Probably Jasen and his mother," replied Savana.

"You are right" Gabriele said, admiring her intuition.

"We just have to ignore them." "I am not married to Jasen but Karolina will probably say something stupid like, "There goes the mother of your son with another man," said Savana sarcastically.

Gabriele laughed really loud. "You sure know about them," said Gabriele.

"Yes, especially Karolina. She is mean and protective of her son. If I had not come into the picture, Jasen would still be waiting for his mother's approval to even talk about marriage," said Savana.

Gabriele arrived to pick up Savana at seven o'clock for dinner. Savana looked very pretty that night and Gabriele just adored her. The restaurant was full and there was a long line outside. The Mediterranean summer breeze made the restaurant's environment warm and cozy. Savana glanced around the corner and she saw Karolina and Jasen looking at her. Savana waved at them and they waved in returned. Gabriele showed his trophy date Savana to their table. Karolina commented to Jasen in her usual snide way, "They sure make a very good-looking couple."

Yes, Jasen agreed like a love lost puppet: "Savana is a beautiful woman. Just take a look at Jerry, as he grows older now; he is just a carbon copy of Savana. He resembles me very little."

Karolina disagreed: "Jerry has your brain. He is a very smart young man like you."

"I wonder if he is going to live with his mother," said Jasen.

Their dinner arrived and there was a note attached to the plate. Karolina took the note and read it. *Your dinner is on the house, Grazia! Gabriele*

"Well, that's very nice of him." "Look! He is coming right now," said Karolina. Gabriele said hello in Sicilian and Karolina said hello back in Sicilian.

"Karolina! You were really young when you came to meet my grandfather in Sicily." They all wanted you to marry my dad," said Gabriele.

"You remembered!" "Yes, they wanted me to marry your dad because I was very pretty but too young to be wise so I married someone else!" Karolina crooned with false modesty.

"I am going to let you enjoy your dinner and we will see you later," said Gabriele. He walked over to Savana and apologized to Savana for talking too long with Karolina and leaving Savana alone.

Chapter Seventeen

"You look very beautiful tonight, Savana," said Gabriele. "When I saw you the first time, I fell in love with you right away. I admired the whole you".

Savana was quiet. "I am attracted to you Gabriele… deeply attracted to you." Savana struggled to say the words closest to her heart. "You are a very handsome man and so kind, so chivalrous- no man has ever helped me like you have. You put me high up on a pedestal of honor and respect and I wonder why I have been so blessed." Savana began to softly weep.

"Let me take you back home now," Gabriele said. Savana lived now about half an hour from the restaurant and neither one spoke until they got home.

"Would you like to come in?" Savana asked hesitantly.

"Yes, I would love to," said Gabriele. The house looked beautiful with all the carpet on the floor even without the furniture.

Gabriele could not resist his urges anymore. He started kissing Savana passionately all over her delicate neck and arms. The light scent of her perfume mingled with the fragrant air and suddenly,

Gabriele found himself making love to Savana and she felt her body yield with every touch of his gentle hands. They both felt happy because they believed it was meant to be.

"Now, I have found my true love, the one woman I have been waiting for, Savana," he whispered. "You are the love of my life." "The first time I saw you, I did not stop thinking about you every night and day. My mind would cry out saying when am I going to see you again?"

Savana responded with a gushing forth of heart felt emotion: "I didn't know that my son was going to take me to your restaurant and when I saw you again, I knew right away that fate brought us together again!".

Gabriele and Savana spent the night on the silk decorative pillows they had arranged on the floor. Gabriele woke up first and remembered the early morning delivery of the custom designed furniture. He told her that he was going to his house to clean up and then he would pick up some Italian pastries and cappuccinos for their breakfast and come back and wait for the furniture with her. Savana was very happy with Gabriele; she believed she had met the man of her dreams.

While waiting for Gabriele to return, Savana gazed out the large front room window overlooking her marble terrace and the Mediterranean Sea. She felt the pink and gold morning mist rising to meet the orgasmic flush of her cheeks and wondered if their romance would last. The delivery of the furniture arrived. Savana was right there to receive it. She showed them where to artistically place each expensive piece of furniture. The house really looked beautiful after they were placed in the right place. The beddings upstairs looked great and they matched the curtains and the rugs. The house looked complete now except for the kitchen. When Gabriele arrived, he complimented Savana: "The house looks beautiful just like you, my love! It looks complete now," he said.

Savana agreed and said, "the kitchen is the only place that needs to be done."

Gabriele agreed. "We can handle that. We can go out and buy the ceramic every day plates and the primo utensils and other top of the line kitchen items," he said. "I am going to check on the restaurant while you put everything together," said Gabriele.

Jerry would be arriving the next week and Savana was really looking forward for her son's arrival. She already made his bedroom with special towels and sheets. She would tell Jasen that Jerry was going to stay with her for a while in Italy.

"I want Jerry to join us in our trip to Sicily next week," said Gabriele.

"That will be really nice," said Savana, "I want him to come closer to the one I care for so completely!".

Gabriele spent the night with Savana and he showed her intimately how much he loved her. He wanted to take her to see his island, Sicily. He wanted to show her how Sicily was so different from Italy.

"Tomorrow, I want us to go to the restaurant and do some work together," he told Savana. They both rose early and got dressed and went to the restaurant. Savana was surprised to see so many Americans and Europeans having breakfast. She remembered that it was summer travel time in Italy -time to enjoy wine tasting and al fresco dining in small seaside and countryside villages. She was thinking that Jasen would be really busy with the vineyard and harvesting his grapes soon, and she was happy that Jerry would be coming to help him with all his newly hired help.

Savana supervised the waitresses and the people who were serving the food from the kitchen where the smell of sautéed garlic filled the air. Mia, one of the cooks, was busy making pasta by hand as the roasted vine-picked tomatoes were simmering with fresh basil in the copper pans. Mia told her that summer was one of their busiest times of the year. They opened up the outside so that people could enjoy the sunny Italian weather. On that day alone, they had more than two hundred guests for breakfast. Savana took a moment to gaze at Gabriele her lover who was very busy with paper work and helping the waiters. Savana noticed how the restaurant business is really physically and mentally demanding. "You have to be strong and willing to work long hours," Savana thought to herself and Savana had no experience at all in the restaurant business. She was tired when the day was over. They were very busy on that day. The summer season is just beginning. They went home very tired. Gabriele was going to stay with Savana until Jerry arrived and then he would return to his house.

"You have a very demanding business Gabriele," said Savana. "I see how busy everyone was. Mia, told me that summer time is one of the busiest times of the year. "Yes, this is when we make a lot of money!" Gabriele happily reported.

"How many restaurants all together do you own and manage?" Savana asked Gabriele.

"I have about ten restaurants and I am going to open two more. The most important thing is to hire the right people to handle the job. Someone who is reliable. Someone who can run the restaurant when I am not there. Someone who I can trust!" explained Gabriele.

Savana understood the success of Gabriele's business model. And she felt very lucky he was her lover. He was so thoughtful and caring too. He told Savana not come in to work the next day but to take care of the house to prepare for Jerry's arrival from college. Many college students were having their summer breaks and they all wanted to travel. He was thinking about Jerry. In just a few days, Jerry would see his mother and they all would be very happy to see each other. Gabriele had been thinking about Savana a lot and he could not wait to ask her to marry him.

Gabriele had already told his dad about his plan to come to Sicily when Jerry arrived. His father was very happy to hear it and told his son Gabriele. "I know Savana is going to love Sicily and the food. She will love the ocean and the weather. I know Jerry is going to love the island as well. I have a feeling that Savana is going to want to stay in Sicily." His father told him that he had been fixing their other home because he had a feeling that Savana might want to stay there. Gabriele thanked his dad and was very happy to hear it.

The day arrived for Jerry to come home. His flight was going to touch down in ten minutes and Savana was waiting for him at the airport. The passengers were coming out one by one and Savana was watching. She finally saw her son and she was so happy and excited. She told her son that he had grown taller. He made a comment to his mother that she looked beautiful and even younger. "Mom, how are my dad and grandma?" he asked.

"They both looked great the last time I saw them. They came and ate at the restaurant." Savana said.

"I am going to visit dad as soon we as we get home," said Jerry.

"I already told your dad that you are going to stay with me and also, we are going to travel to Sicily with Gabriele before you are going to work for your dad at his *Paradiso* vineyard," Savana told Jerry.

Her son liked her house and he walked upstairs to look at his bedroom and unpack. He was happy to be reunited with his mother and to share all his amazing college experiences with her. He told his mother that he missed her a lot. Savana drove Jerry to see his dad and he was surprised to see him.

"You are beginning to be a very handsome young man, Jerry," his faither said. "Your mother told me that after you return from Sicily then you can come and join my workforce. "

Chapter
Eighteen

On a Monday morning the three of them took the first flight to Sicily. It was really a very short flight. Bruno was waiting for them at the airport. "Hi dad!" said Gabriele. Meet Savana and Jerry!" He introduced them to his dad.

"Jerry, look at you, you grew up so fast. I heard that you're going to school in America now," said Bruno.

"Yes, I am on summer break now and I am going to work for my dad at his new *Paradiso* vineyard," said Jerry.

"I am very happy to meet you Savana and I hope you enjoy Sicily during your visit," said Bruno. He drove them to his house out in the country.

Savana and Jerry enjoyed the scenery and the ocean. They all hopped out from the vehicle and took their luggage into the house. They got along great with all Gabriele's relatives. Jerry was very happy to see his mother finally truly happy. They prepared a very big feast for everybody. Gabriele's mother walked in and Gabriele proudly introduced Savana to his mother. She was very happy to meet her. Savana really felt welcome here. Gabriele had a quick conversation with his dad telling him that he was going to propose to Savana right then and there. This was going to be a big surprise to Savana and Jerry. Gabriele took out the ring and went straight to Savana and went down on his knees and asked Savana to marry him. Savana cried and Jerry also couldn't hide his joy. "Yes! Yes! I will marry you!" cried Savana. Gabriele tenderly kissed her and Jerry came and kissed his mother with tears in his eyes.

"You really surprised my mother, Gabriele," Jerry said with joy. "She thought we just came here for a vacation and little did she know that it was bigger than that. Thank you for honoring my mother. She has not been treated very well by my grandmother and because of my grandmother's negative feelings, my dad refused to marry my mother. They made her feel so unwanted in their house.

"I think about her all the time and I am very happy that she moved out from that house," Jerry confessed.

"I know that they were not treating her very well. She looked sad all the time and I knew that something was wrong," said Gabriele.

Jerry confided to Gabriele: "Mom was ready to go back to America because of me. But I wanted her to be happy and I wanted her to meet someone who was able and willing to make her happy. Thank you very much for proposing marriage to her. Mom is a wonderful person. And we are looking forward to joining your large Sicilian family!"

Gabriele had two sisters and two brothers. He also owned a restaurant and a bar near the ocean. He was going to take Savana and Jerry to see it in the morning. Bruno told them that the restaurant had been doing very well. There were many tourists and the beach was full of sun worshipers, boaters and surf boarders.

"Do you know how to swim, Savana?" asked Bruno.

"Yes, I love to swim!" replied Savana. "Jerry knows how to swim too," she said.

"Gabriele has a big boat that we are going sailing on tomorrow," said Bruno.

Gabriele woke up early that morning and went straight to the restaurant. It was 8 a.m. when he arrived and the restaurant had begun to get filled up. He looked out on the patio and observed how many people already sat out there.

"Most people take their vacations to come here. Sicily has very beautiful weather in the summer," said Bruno. They all sat down and had their tasty freshly cooked breakfast.

"This is a beautiful restaurant," said Jerry.

"My son is not into vineyards and grapes. He is into restaurants and bars," said Bruno.

Gabriele came and joined them outside. They were getting ready to go down to Gabriele's large pristine white yacht. Savana noticed many people were swimming and surfing.

"Did you bring your swimming suit Savana?" asked Gabriele.

"Yes, I did."

The sun shine was warm enough for sun bathing. The boat was anchored in the deep end of the ocean. They were picked up by one of Gabriele workers in a small boat to take them to the yacht. The summer weather was very nice to Savana. Jerry could not keep his eyes away from his mother. She looked very happy and calm.

"Why are you staring at me, Jerry?" his mother asked.

"I am just admiring you mom; how beautiful you look. You look happy and vibrant," said Jerry.

Savana just smiled at him. She was really happy that Jerry was there with her. They reached the 300-foot yacht. They all got on the yacht and Gabriele led them down stairs to show them their rooms where they would be spending the night. Jerry loved his bedroom right next to his mom's. Gabriele was around the corner from them. His dad and his mother were right down from him. He showed them the kitchen where about fifteen people were working with two chefs. They were busy preparing the lunch and breakfast.

The dining area was next to the kitchen but Gabriele told them that everyone was going to eat upstairs so they could enjoy the summer weather. The boat had a big swimming pool where they could go swimming or they could choose to slide down to swim in the ocean.

Gabriele and Savana had decided to get married in December when Jerry would be home for Christmas. They told Jerry and he was very happy for both of them. The view of the turquoise green sea was very beautiful. Savana and Jerry just sat there on chairs and looked out. They watched the sunset blazing aflame before the sun settled down to sleep on the pinkish orange horizon. A cool Mediterranean Sea breeze blew Savana's long soft brown hair and golden light from the sunset shone through her silken hair. Afterwards, they all took showers and changed into their summer evening clothes.

Savana wore a beautiful white dress just suitable for the summer weather and Jerry wore a light blue shirt and a pair of white shorts. Gabriele wore a pair of light blue shorts and a white shirt. Gabriele admired how beautiful Savana looked while she gazed with pride on her only son.

"My son, you look very handsome tonight, and you've grown up so fast!" cried Savana. "You too Gabriele! This summer weather makes you look like a tanned godlike Sicilian!" said Savana laughing.

They all sat around the table with Bruno and Mia, Gabriele's parents. The dinner was served- a very traditional Sicilian dish which is called "Pasta alle Norma" made from local tomatoes, eggplant, garlic, basil, pasta and ricotta, salute cheese. Amidst the clinking of wine glasses, the moon over the ocean was shining on the deck of the yacht and bathing the ocean in silver. Gabriele told Savana he could be spending most of the day at the restaurant. "You can all go and do some shopping with my mom or Jerry can check out the different vineyards with my dad or go swimming in the ocean or come with me to the restaurant," said Gabriele.

"I want to go with you Gabriele- this way we will know each other better," said Jerry.

"I am glad that you are coming with me, Jerry," said Gabriele. "This will help you with your school work towards achieving your business degree."

Jerry was happy to help Gabriele at the restaurant.

The restaurant like the moon was full. It was summer time and everyone was hungry and thirsty. Jerry helped Gabriele with his paper work. Gabriele thanked him before they left to go and see his mother. He saw his mother was swimming with Gabriele's parents and noticed she was very happy and laughing and talking with them. He was very happy to see his mother happy. They had planned to stay in Sicily until the end of summer. Now it was time for them to return to Italy.

Jerry excused himself to go to bed and told them he would see them in the morning. They said "Grazia e arrivederci! to Gabriele's parents, and reminded them about the wedding in December.

Chapter
Twenty

Waiting for the first flight back to Italy, Jerry' father called him. He wanted to see Jerry right away. He went to see his father at the vineyard. Jasen was very happy to see his son. "You look good son! How was Sicily? "

"Sicily was beautiful and I want to tell you about our great news, dad. Gabriele proposed to mom and they are going to get married in December in Sicily!" Jerry told his father.

Oh! That is great news," said Jasen. "Your grandmother is going to be here very soon and make sure you tell her the good news," said Jasen.

"Where is my grandson?" asked Karolina.

"I am here grandma," said Jerry.

Karolina was very glad to see him. "How was Sicily?" asked Karolina.

"I really had a good time and we were able to enjoy Gabriele's beautiful yacht. We sailed out to the ocean and went swimming. There were so many people on the beach. Gabriele certainly has his restaurant located at the right place. I went with him to help work at his restaurant and it was just packed with people from all over the world. I met his parents and relatives too. They were very nice people. Grandma, I have to tell you very good news. Gabriele has proposed to mom to marry her."

"When is the wedding?" asked Karolina.

"In December when I have my winter break," said Jerry. Karolina was very happy to hear the news. They went to meet his father for lunch.

On the way, Jerry's phone rang and it was his mother. He told her that he was just about to have lunch with Jasen and his grandma. Savana told him to go ahead and have lunch and she would see him at home. Karolina started telling Jasen the secrets about Gabriele's family. "His family is very wealthy. Your grandfather told me about them. They don't want to marry people that don't have any money. It is funny that he picked Savana to marry."

"Maybe he saw something in her that opened his heart. Savana is a very beautiful person and he decided to marry her," said Jasen defensively.

"Let's not tell Jerry or his mother about our secret," said Karolina.

"Well mama, eventually they will hear or know of Gabriele's true wealth and the family's bias." You can't hide family secrets-eventually someone will know," said Jasen. 'I know Savana as an American will really laugh when she hears about this socio-economic bias. She will make fun of it," Jasen told his mother.

"However, I have a problem with Savana's wedding in December," Jasen complained. "Sofi is three months pregnant and as soon as Jerry finds out, he will tell his mother," Jasen remarked.

Karolina responded with a hidden strategy: "We will not tell them yet. Jerry is leaving for school next week and that should give us time to plan your wedding." Karolina added: "Savana is getting married in December and by that time, Sofi should have her baby."

"I still think we should tell them now before they know it later. You always keep everything as a secret mama and I don't like it," said Jasen.

Jerry already had his lunch and he told his father that he was going home to see his mother. She wanted to do something with him. "I will see you over the weekend" he told his father. As soon as he got home, he told his mother that his grandmother, Karolina and his dad looked very quiet and very calm.

"They both asked me about Sicily and I told them how amazing the people are. Also, how impressed I was with their yacht and the ocean. I broke the news to them that you and Gabriele are going to get married in December. They both were happy and excited to hear the news. "Mom, they are definitely hiding something, and whatever it is -it will come out."

Karolina keeps everything secret especially when it comes to your dad," said Savana.

"I am going back there this weekend and I will make sure that I keep my eyes on him," said Jerry.

"I might come with you. I haven't seen your dad for a long time and I need to talk to him too," said Savana. "Do you know if he has girlfriend now? Karolina always wanted your dad to marry an Italian girl. I remember when they came to Italy when I was pregnant with you; he fell in love with one girl and he decided he was not going to marry me. He brought me and you with them here. I think your grandmother stopped him from marrying me," Savana said with a somewhat bitter tone. "We were supposed to get married when we got here but something happened. Karolina said something to your father to stop our marriage!" she said.

"Mother, I am glad- you made the right choice to marry Gabriele and he is nice; he is young and has a lot of money. I am glad that you are not marrying dad. Karolina will always cause problems with you saying that you are not good enough for dad. I told dad that you are going to marry Gabriele; he looked surprised and sad. I think their Italian culture always wants to marry their own kind."

"Yes, that is very true. Karolina always thinks that I am not good enough for your dad and that he should marry an Italian woman."

"Your dad always listens to his mother. He will never go against her at all and that's why we are not together today. I am not going to keep waiting for him to make up his mind. I need to move on. I am not any younger and I need to enjoy my life," said Savana.

"I am happy for you mom because you found someone who really loves you and cares about you," said Jerry.

"I am very proud of you Jerry. You've grown up to be a very smart boy and a handsome boy too!" They both laughed at one another. Gabriele told them to come and have dinner at the restaurant with him that evening. They got dressed and left for the restaurant.

Gabriele was very busy when they arrived. The waitress led them to the table that Gabriele reserved for them. Finally, Gabriele came said sat down at their table and said hello to them. He asked them what they had been doing. Jerry said that he went to see his dad and he asked him how was Sicily and he told him that you are marrying my mom in December.

"How did he take it?" asked Gabriele.

"He was surprised -actually he could not believe it," said Jerry. Jerry told him that he felt like they were hiding something. "They stayed very calm after I shared Mom's marriage announcement and they were happy to hear more news about you and mom but of course, my grandmother always seems to have some kind of secret inside her head." Both Savana and Gabriele laughed.

Chapter Twenty-One

Savana agreed and said that Karolina knows many secrets and of course she must have known secrets about Gabriele's family too.

"She knows everyone's secrets and my dad knew some secrets about his family too," said Gabriele. He was going to ask his dad to come and tell the secrets about Karolina's family.

"My grandfather was a very good friend with Karolina's father. They used to visit each other and dine together. They would go to Sicily and spend weeks at my grandfather's vineyard. "They are very wealthy people," said Gabriele.

"That's why she doesn't allow my dad to marry mom," Jerry commented. "It is sad that my grandmother feels that way. She wants my father to marry an Italian woman with money too," said Jerry.

"Not necessarily, she wants Jasen to marry an Italian to keep the blood line pure. Savana is an outsider. She does not have any money or social status either. Jasen is an educated man and a doctor as well. She figured that her son deserved someone better," explained Gabriele.

"My mom went to college also and graduated too. She has a degree in English. My mom does not talk about this. My grandmother has no idea about my mom. My mom does not go around and tell everyone. My father knew about it," said Jerry.

"I can teach English here," said Savana.

"My mom will tell you a lot of things that you still don't know Gabriele," said Jerry. "I went to see dad this morning and they both asked me about Sicily. I told them that I had a nice time." They were very calm. I felt they were hiding something from me. I had to let them know that you proposed to my mother. I saw my dad look sad but my grandmother was happy. I went to get something to eat and I saw them talking about something. They could not believe that you proposed to my mom. I know deep down my father is still in love with my mom, but his mother was blocking him. I don't like the way they are treating my mom and especially my grandmother. She looked at my mother like she is nothing and not good enough for my father. She thinks that my father is well educated and he is a doctor and he deserves somebody better. She does know that my mom went to college and graduated and she has a degree in English. My dad knows that. When I saw them this morning, they behaved differently. They looked like they were hiding something from me. I went to get something to eat. On my way back, they were talking about something and they stopped talking when I arrived."

"I am going to tell both of you now, mom is going to call me to say that dad is getting married," Jerry said half joking. They all laughed. "Let's stop talking about them. Maybe we will hear something before I go back to school," said Jerry.

"Let us go home and sleep." said Gabriele.

Jasen called Jerry the next day and asked him if he wanted to come and have breakfast with him. This will be the last week you can spend with me Jerry."

"Yes dad. I would love to come and have breakfast with you," he told his father.

He called his mother and told her the news. His mother was happy for Jerry to go and spend time with his father before he left for school again. He got dressed and left to see his father.

Chapter Twenty-Two

Karolina was there to have breakfast with them. "I am very happy to see you Jerry and how is your mother?" asked Karolina.

"She is home and she's doing very well."

"Hi dad. How are you on this fantastic morning?" asked his son.

"I am doing great and feeling well," said Jasen. "Are you ready to go back to school?"

"Yes," replied Jerry. "It has been a fun summer and I really enjoyed it. I apologize for not really helping you dad but I was glad that I got to know Gabriele. He is a wonderful guy and he is really good for mom!" Jerry told his father and grandmother Karolina.

"When are they getting married?" asked Karolina.

"In December when I come to visit for Christmas break. They are getting married in Sicily," said Jerry. There was a long pause between them. "Mom wanted to come and join us for breakfast this morning," said Jerry.

"You should have asked her to come. We have not seen her for a long time," said Karolina.

"We'll ask her if she wants to join us for lunch tomorrow," said Jasen. Karolina did not say anything. "Jerry, tell your mother to come and have lunch with us tomorrow."

Jerry went home and left his dad and Karolina behind.

"Mom, dad invited us to come and have lunch with them tomorrow," said Jerry.

"How was your breakfast?" Savana asked Jerry.

It was very nice and grandma was there also and she was happy to see me. She asked about you," said Jerry. "I will go with you tomorrow to have lunch with your dad."

They went out shopping for some new clothes for Jerry. "Did your dad give you some money?" asked Savana.

"Yes, he did!" replied Jerry. "Karolina gave me some money also. Savana burst out laughing.

"How much?" Savana asked.

"You will be very surprised to hear that it is about five hundred euro," said Jerry.

"Karolina is a funny grandmother, when she does things like that. She probably wanted to know something or she knows something she does not want to tell." Savana said. "Bribery is a form of control for her.

"Mom, you know the manipulations of my grandmother very well!"

"I've lived with them for a very long time" Savana replied. "Your dad would have married me without her vindictive plot," said Savana.

"I know mom. You and dad were really in love. He turned down all those beautiful Italian women because he was in love with you," said Jerry.

"I know, he is very thankful that he made me pregnant so he could have a child. I know, he is very happy to see you growing up to be very smart boy just like him."

"Dad told me that he missed me very much and that I always make him happy when he sees me. I told him, dad, I will come whenever you want to see me or need me to help as well," said Jerry. "I think he is going to tell us something tomorrow," said Jerry. His mother agreed . "When does Gabriele finish work tonight?" Jerry asked his mother.

"At eight p.m. Savana replied. They finished their shopping and went home. Savana grilled some fish they brought back from Sicily and prepared mashed potatoes and salad. "This is an America way of cooking. No pasta!" said Savana.

Chapter
Twenty-Three

Gabriele arrived and he brought their dinner. "Are you eating already?"

"Yes, American style!" Savana said with a smile.

Gabriele laughed. "Well, I brought Italian food," he said.

They all had dinner and Savana told him about the lunch with Jasen and Karolina. Gabriele said that probably they were going to reveal something to them.

"We will wait and see what they are going to tell us," Jerry replied.

"Maybe a woman is pregnant and Karolina wants Jasen to get married quickly before it becomes public knowledge," Gabriele said. Knowing Karolina, she will tell Jasen not to tell the truth," Gabriele said, slightly smirking.

"You are probably right. She knows a lot of secrets about anybody and anything," said Savana. They all went to bed and the house was all quiet.

In the morning, Gabriele left for work at 7am, and Savana rose early to make a healthy breakfast for Jerry. Jerry woke and told his mom again how much he loved her and missed her while he was attending college. Then he asked her questions about Gabriele who would soon become his step-father.

"Does he want to have children, Mom?"

"We haven't really discussed about having a family because he is very busy right now. Maybe when the summer season is over and things are slowing down," said Savana. "By the way, Jerry, I am scheduled to have lunch with your grandmother and Jasen this afternoon."

Karolina was happy to see Savana for lunch.

"You look very well Karolina," said Savana. Karolina said the same thing to Savana. Jasen was also very happy to see Savana. "How was Sicily?" he asked.

"A truly beautiful Island," she replied.

"Congratulations to both of you. Are getting married to Gabriele in December,?" he asked.

"Yes, we are. We are going to Sicily to get married there. His family are very nice people," Savana said.

"Yes, they are", His grandfather was a good friend with my grandfather," Jasen said.

"Gabriele told me the story," she said. "He has been really busy after we came back from Sicily and he is going to be travelling next year to open up several restaurants in Europe and the United States," she told Jasen. "Are you going with him?" he asked.

"We have not discussed anything yet. I want to go and see my parents in California when he opens a restaurant in Napa," she said.

"I have something here for you, dad and grandma," Jerry told his father.

Karolina opened her present and she was very happy when she saw her beautiful white scarf and her white sweater. She thanked Jerry.

Jasen opened his present and he was surprised to see his beautiful blue shirt and his blue tie. He thanked his son. They ate their lunch and everyone was quiet and finally, Jasen spoke up. He had something to tell them. "I am going to open up a clinic here in Italy.

"Wow" that's great dad. You are going to be very busy," said Jerry.

"I will have four doctors working with me. I just bought another house. I just sold the old one."

"Where are you going to have the clinic?" asked Jerry.

"Not very far away from here" Jasen said.

"We are very happy for you and wish you great success," Savana said.

"Dad are you ever going to get married?" Jerry blurted out.

"You keep asking me this question," he said laughing at the same time.

"No Jerry. Your dad has not found any woman yet," said Karolina answering for her grown son.

"What kind of woman do you like grandma?" asked Jerry. "It looks like you are blocking dad from getting married. My dad is getting old now and very soon he is going to be too old to get married," said Jerry.

"You have been listening to your mom too long," said Karolina.

"My mom has not told me anything. It is pretty obvious that you do not want my dad to get married!" Jerry answered feeling his rage rising.

"How dare you talk to me like that. Your dad can make up his mind and he can choose any woman he likes!" yelled Karolina.

"You did not want my dad to marry my mom!" Jerry shouted back, "because you didn't think she was good enough to marry my dad!"

"I want both of you to leave right now. I don't want to see both of you!" screamed Karolina turning red in the face.

"I am very proud of my son to tell you the truth. You are a very selfish old lady. You want your son for you and you alone. Release him and let him find a woman before it is too late!" Savana said with a stern strained voice. They said goodbye to Jasen and they left in a huff.

Jerry was crying and feeling sorry for his dad. "How dare she chase me out in front of my dad. She really controls my dad."

"I am very proud of you son; you confronted Karolina and she needed that. She couldn't believe that you said that to her," said Savana.

"I am not weak like my father. I am definitely different from him," said Jerry. They went home and talked about what happened. Gabriele was waiting for them.

"How was the dinner?" asked Gabriele.

"Karolina chased us out," said Jerry.

"Why? What was the reason?" Gabriele asked in shock.

"Jerry confronted her about holding his dad and controlling him," Savana blurted out.

"She is a tough woman and she wants her son to possess money and high class," Gabriele tried to explain. "Her family is related to the king of Italy. That's why she is behaving like that. The main purpose is to keep the money in the family. She looked at you Savana with harsh biased judgement and she decided that you are not worthy of her son," said Gabriele.

"She told us to leave," said Jerry. "I am not like my dad at all. He cannot face my grandma. She controls everything, including the vineyard," he said.

"Oh yes, she is always trying to control everything and her husband listened to her all the time," explained Gabriele.

"I still think they are hiding something. I saw my dad just about ready to say something and Karolina said something else to block it," said Jerry. His mother agreed too. She had a feeling that Jasen was just about to tell them something.

"This is my advice to you, please do not go back and see them," Gabriele pleaded. I am glad you are going back to school and I am going to have your mom to come and do some work in the restaurant," Gabriele said.

Jerry added: "They sold the old house and bought another one. We forgot to tell you; my dad has opened his own clinic with four others doctors.

"Really," Gabriele responded surprised, "that tells me that your dad is settling down here and that he is ready to get married. Maybe the woman is pregnant," said Gabriele.

"You know what I almost asked my dad that question. I think you are right. I think the woman is pregnant. Very interesting," said Jerry.

"That is going to be one of Karolina's biggest secrets. He may be planning to marry the women fast before news of her pregnancy gets out!" conjectured Gabriele.

Chapter Twenty-Four

"We are very consumed with Karolina's secrets and who knows what's up her sleeve now," said Savana.

Exhausted, Gabriele and Savana went to bed but Jerry was up for a while. He did not like how Karolina treated him that night. Jerry was a very strong young man and he was not going to take that type of rude treatment just because they thought they were better than anyone else. He loves his mother and he is going to protect her and he has witnessed how Karolina treated his mother and he is not going to allow Karolina or anyone else to treat her like that. He decided to talk with his dad tomorrow. He went to sleep that night thinking about Karolina and he was awakened by his mom's knock on his door.

"Do you know what time it is, Jerry?" his mother asked.

"I stayed up late last night and I just could not go to sleep. I was thinking how cruel Karolina treated us yesterday. I am going to go and talk with dad today." "What time is it mom?" he asked.

"It is 1 pm," she said. Jerry told his mom that he was sorry that he overslept. He called his dad and asked him if he could see him. His dad was worried about this crisis and said yes of course!" He quickly drove to his vineyard and he saw his father was waiting for him.

"What's up son?" Jasen asked.

"I want to talk with you about grandma. She chased us out last night, which was very rude. She has no respect for anyone at all. Dad, you are weak, you cannot even face your own mother. You just let her run your own life. She is old now, and she should listen to you. She never wanted my mother to marry you. My mother was not good enough for you. Just look at you! You are almost sixty years old now and still not married. You need to stop listening to her," Jerry told his dad with his anger and frustration rising. "I feel bad for both you and mom. I know, you still love my mom very much. But what did grandma do? She separated both you. Mom cries sometimes when she thinks about you but she cannot do anything now. Gabriele is a wonderful man and he loves mom. He wants the best for mom. They are very close with their age groups. Mom and he will be travelling together next year and she will go to see her parents and friends as well," Jerry said to his dad.

"Your grandma is like this all the time and you cannot argue with her," Jasen said trying to make excuses for his mother's outrageous behavior. "When your grandpa was still alive, she used to treat him like this all the time. I think it is the way she was brought up. Everything was given to her on a silver platter. She did whatever she wanted when she wanted and she was really spoiled by her parents. Her mother was related to the King of Italy," said Jasen.

"She is still bringing that royalty treatment expectation with her," said Jerry. "We are living in the twentieth century now dad, but she thinks that we are living in the seventeenth century! She thinks she's the queen of Italy! She treats my mom like a slave," he complained. "She has to change her life style. Last night she didn't even have a conversation with my mom. What was that all about?" Jerry asked in disgust. "I better go back and see what mom is doing. We are supposed to go last minute shopping today," said Jerry. "Well, dad I better say goodbye now and I look forward to seeing you during Christmas break."

Before Jasen could respond, Jerry noticed this woman was walking quickly towards them. She looked pregnant. "Oh, this must be your son! I better go back until you finish your conversation," she said in an anxious tone.

"Come back Sophia -we are just saying good bye," Jerry said shocked and annoyed. Jerry was the last person Jasen wanted to see Sophia-the woman Jasen was going to marry and who was also carrying his child. Jasen knew that Jerry was very smart and observant and he would put things together and surmise that this beautiful Italian woman was carrying his dad's baby.

Jerry left for home and he couldn't wait to deliver the news to his mom.

"Hi Mom! I am sorry I'm late. Karolina was not there and I ended up talking to dad instead. He explained everything to me about Karolina and the reasons for her outrageous behavior."

Terry reported to his mother all the strange details of his meeting with Jasen, his father. "I explained to him that we are not living in the seventeenth century now. We are not living in a time where money determines your social status. He told me that I should forgive her. She is getting old and most of the time she does not mean what she speaks. But just as I was about to leave, a very big surprise happened. Dad was not expecting this at all. This beautiful Italian woman came rushing over to dad and was surprised to see me. She wanted to go back but I told her that I was just leaving. The woman looked about three months pregnant. I looked at dad's eyes and observed he did not like the scene. I excused myself and left. I am sure that is his baby and they are keeping it as a secret and that is why they sold the house and bought another house because the woman is going to have his child."

"That must be why he decided to practice medicine again too," Savana surmised. "Your dad knew that you are very smart son. If you come and tell me, we will put everything together and we will come up with the right answer," Savana stated.

Gabriele was right all the time. He knew Karolina's family very well. They are going to find out real soon the story behind the woman Jerry saw.

"Now we can move on and all these secrets and the vineyards are all behind us now. I feel like something has been lifted from me and now I feel very happy that I am free at last. I can laugh and talk," said Savana.

"I am so proud of you mom. All along, I saw that you were not happy and something was holding you back even though you are with Gabriele now. I felt there was something deep inside you holding you back. Now, we found the answer. Your wonderful smile has come back now and that happy feeling you always have that was taken away from you is back again!" said Jerry with happy tears in his eyes.

"Why don't we go and surprise Gabriele at the restaurant?" said Savana.

"Wow! Mom, I never have seen you so excited before like this," said Jerry. Savana exclaimed: "I just feel very strong and free and thank God for always watching over us. God always works in a mysterious way. He saw that Karolina was mistreating me and saw me not saying bad things back, and he turned around and blessed me. I am happy that I have you son and I am happy that we kept it as a secret from Karolina!" Savana said reverently."

"But God was protecting you all the time and he knew that this was going to happen," said Jerry.

Gabriele was surprised to see Savana and Jerry. He was very happy to see both of them. "Ciao Bella! Hello Beautiful!" "What a big surprise to see both of you! I was going to call you to bring Jerry over since he is going back to school next week. It would be nice to bring him and have dinner with us," said Gabriele.

"Well, here we are, and we have something to tell you," Savana said. "Jerry decided to go and have lunch with Jasen. He wanted to face Karolina because he did not like what she did to us the previous day. Unfortunately, she was not there. Jerry talked with his dad instead and told him what he thought about Karolina. His father explained to him why Karolina often behaves the way she does. Jerry stood up and was ready to leave when he saw this woman rapidly walking over to his dad. Jasen looked surprised to see her. Jerry noticed that she was pregnant. "

Savana continued to relay this scandalous revelation. Jerry excused himself from the conversation and left. Jerry knew right away that must be the woman dad is going to marry. They have been hiding this pregnancy from us and Karolina wants them to get married before we know," explained Savana. "Gabriele, everything you have been telling us is true."

"Like I already told you, Gabriele emphasized, that's why they bought another house and he decided to open his practice. I am sure that woman works at the vineyard or is someone who has a lot of money. Karolina won't allow Jasen to marry any woman who has no money. The woman he marries should be just like her.

Chapter Twenty-Six

"Karolina's family is very wealthy and they can buy the whole city if they want. That is the very reason why Jasen is very loyal to his mother. If he is disloyal to her, she will cut him off from the family inheritance," Gabriele said, shaking his head in disgust.

"My dad does not need the family money; he has his own money and he does not need this old money from Karolina," Jerry replied in a defensive mode.

"I am very proud of you Jerry; you are not like your father at all. You are very strong and smart." That is from my side of the family. Both of my parents are attorneys and my brother is still in law school," Savana argued with pride.

"That was my first choice," said Jerry. "I can do both. A business man and a lawyer!"

Do you have any plans for tomorrow?" Gabriele asked Jerry.

I already packed my clothes and I am ready to go back to school," said Jerry.

"Let's go down to the beach. I want to show you where Karolina's family used to live. She still has some relatives living there," Gabriele suggested.

They all left to go home. Jasen called Jerry as soon as they got home.

"Dad is calling me. Hi dad," said Jerry.

"I just want to apologize to you about what happened today. I was not expecting Sofi to interrupt us like that. She didn't know who you were and I had to explain the situation to her," said Jasen.

"Who was that woman?" asked Jerry suspiciously.

"She is just someone who works at the vineyard," Jasen answered in a flat tone showing no emotion.

"Is she one of the mangers at the vineyard. Is she pregnant?" asked Jerry.

"Yes, she is," Jasen quickly answered brushing off any implications or further questions.

Quickly changing the subject, Jasen asked his son, "What time is your flight on Monday?"

"My flight is at 10 am one way to New York and then I transfer to another flight to Boston. I should be in Harvard by Tuesday morning. "

"That's a very long flight!" Jasen said. "I am not going to see you, but I've enjoyed our short time together. I love you very much son and don't forget to call me when you feel like talking."

"Thanks Dad and I love you very much too!"

Chapter
Twenty-Seven

Gabriel overheard Jerry's parting conversation with his father and he wanted to communicate some element of truth to Jerry. "Jerry, Jasen knows that Savana and I are getting married in December. This mystery women Sofia will be having her baby sometime in December. They should be getting married soon. That's why she was hurrying to see Jasen. She wants to talk about the wedding," said Gabriele with compassion in his voice.

"You are right!" Savana uttered disdainfully.

"We are going to receive the wedding invitations soon. I am just wondering what Karolina is thinking right now."

"Is she afraid that all her secrets will be revealed now? She reminds me of an old devil. She is guarding her forbidden fruit who is her own son, Savana commented curtly.

As far as Savana concerned, Karolina's secrets always hung ripe on the Italian family vine waiting to be stomped into intoxicating but poisonous blood-red wine.

"Let's go to bed now before we conjure up the old witch and have nightmares!" Gabriele' said half joking and half mocking.

Jerry stayed up again thinking about his father. He remembered his mother telling him what happened one day when she was pregnant with him. His father and Karolina went to Italy for a vacation. With his usual passion for beautiful women, his dad fell in love with two Italian women. He remembered his mother telling him the name of one of them was "Sofi" and now it all made sense to him. He wondered if his mom still remembered any of this. He decided to talk to her in the morning.

Then he heard a knock on his door. He opened the door and there was his mom. She could not go to sleep either and she saw Jerry's light was still on, so she decided to come over.

"Mom you just arrived at the right time," he said. "I am sitting here thinking about dad. I feel sorry for him to be Karolina's hostage or her forbidden fruit. It seems like Karolina always savors the last sip of her forbidden wine. Do you still remember telling me about dad. He fell in love with two beautiful Italian women when you were pregnant with me? One was named Sofi. I saw her today and she looked pregnant Do you remember that mom?" asked Jerry.

"You have a very good memory, Jerry. I remember both names, one was Sofi and the other one was Gabriella. This one's name is Sofi and she is pregnant. So, I think they are getting married soon," said Savana. "This is Karolina's secret. I bet you that she is not going to invite us to this exclusive Italian wedding and I don't really care. Let's see what else she is going to lie about!"

Jerry decided to share another thought that was on his heart. "Business is really easy for me to study, mom. I am going to be done with school in the next three semesters, then I am going to study law right after that. I haven't talked to dad yet, but I am sure he will agree," Jerry announced to Savana with absolute certainty.

"Your American grandfather is a criminal attorney and one of the best in the states of California" said Savana. I am going to miss you mom!' said Jerry. 'I want you to stay strong and don't let anyone tell you what to do," said Savana.

"I am going back to help Gabriele at the restaurant," Savana said warmly and enthusiastically. "Gabriele will protect me and keep me strong!"

Jerry was taking off at 10 a.m sharp on Monday morning. Jerry and Savana arrived early at the airport that morning and sat down and waited. His phone rang and it was his dad.

"Good morning dad! You surprised me," said Jerry.

"I just had to call to say goodbye again to you son. Have a safe journey and study hard. Wishing you all the best at school and see you in December," said Jasen.

"Thank you, dad, and I wish you the same. Good bye until Christmas break."

Jerry told his mother that his father did not sound happy. He did not tell him about the woman Sofi or when he was going to be married.

"Mom, we do not even know if Sofia is really pregnant by dad. We are just assuming," he told his mother hoping it wasn't true.

"Believe me it is true. That's how Karolina operates. These are her secrets. The next two weeks we are going to hear that Jasen got married and that they had a private wedding," said Savana confidently.

They announced Jerry's flight and he said good bye to his teary mom. "I will call you when I arrive in school," said Jerry.

Savana went immediately to see Gabriele at the restaurant. He noticed that she had been crying. He told her to go home and relax and he would come and meet her there for lunch. He was not going back to work. He decided to take Savana for a drive. Savana arrived home and cleaned Jerry's room, but it was already very clean. She laughed and felt happy that Jerry was growing up to be a very responsible boy, and she was very proud of him. She had been looking for wedding dresses for her Christmas wedding and she was planning to go and check some stores out.

Gabriele arrived to have lunch with her. He decided to take her out to this beautiful restaurant near the Mediterranean Sea. The weather was beginning to get cooler. They arrived at the restaurant and they were happy the restaurant was not full nor the beach. All the tourists and vacationers had gone home. They had a very quiet lunch. Savana watched the waves washing on the white sandy beach. She felt melancholy like a wave crashing into her heart with a loneliness for her son.

"Why have been so quiet today?" asked Gabriele.

"I am just thinking about Jerry. You know, I went to look at his room and it was really clean and everything is in order and I was really surprised," said Savana.

"We should not worry about Jerry too much. He is a very smart young man. I was listening to him- the way he talked about Karolina and how he wanted to straighten her out. He is very strong and very different from his father. He is very out spoken and I agree he should study to be a lawyer. He is going to be a good one," said Gabriele. "Let us talk about ourselves and our relationship and future together now that Jerry has left for school." We should start preparing our wedding celebration. We are going to Sicily next month to get everything ready. We are going to have the ceremony in our boat lit with joyful Christmas lights. And we will sail down the ocean with our mast decorated like a Christmas tree and our hearts filled with hope and love," Gabriele said with a sincere smile.

Savana had been looking for a special wedding dress with pearls from the local seashore and yards of authentic antique Italian lace. She told Gabriele about her vision and he happily handed her his credit card to realize her dreams.

"Let's go look around together at different stores and if you like something, just tell them. These boutique store owners know me, so don't be afraid to ask for anything," Gabriele offered with his whole heart beating solely for his Bella Savana.

They arrived at his favorite store and Gabriele introduced Savana to the store owner and told her that Savana needed some female help to find the perfect wedding dress. Gabriele reiterated that cost was no problem-whatever made his blushing bride happy! The owner/designer smiled at Savana and asked Savana what style she wanted. Savana explained the style she envisioned: A traditional white lacy dress with a pearl and diamond encrusted V back and front . Long sleeves ending in a delicate V on each hand also encrusted with diamonds and pearls and a long gown gathered at her tiny waist and flowing down from the V in graceful waves sprinkled with diamonds and pearls. Savana added that the V was a symbol for Viva Amore and new beginnings.

The owner of the wedding boutique store laughed and then took her measurements and noted exactly her style and size. She wrapped it up quickly before Gabriele arrived.

"It would be bad luck if he saw her perfect dress before the ceremony," she earnestly explained.

"Have you found your dream dress?" Gabriele asked.

"Yes, I found a beautiful wedding dress," replied Savana.

"Oh! You already had it wrapped up!" said Gabriele.

"Yes, we had to wrap it up quickly before you arrived. It will be bad luck if you see it before the wedding," said the owner of the store.

They all laughed.

"You are superstitious people," said Gabriele.

Chapter
Twenty-Nine

As they continued shopping down the village's exclusive shopping lane, Gabriele bought some perfume and a dress for Savana. He bought a pair of shoes for himself. They drove back home and Jerry already called her. He called again and spoke with his mom.

"How was your flight back to school?" asked Savana.

"It was very nice because I slept all the way." Jerry said.

"In December, when you get home, I will take you over to the village boutique. You will love the store and all the things they sell. They are quite expensive, but we can just look around until we find the perfectly tailored wool suit for you, Jerry. Of course, you will be Gabriel's best man and son- to- be during the ceremony!" laughed Savana.

"I am glad that Gabriele is spending some of his time with you," said Jerry.

"We will be spending more time together soon. We are going to Sicily next month to prepare for our wedding. We will be having our honeymoon in the yacht. He is talking about sailing to some exotic islands north of Sicily. I believe they are called the Aeolian Islands and some are even famous for their black volcanic sand beaches," explained Savana.

"Sounds really good mom," Jerry expressed with sincerity.

"I have been having strange dreams lately, Savana confessed. I dreamt that Gabriele has a secret girlfriend and Karolina knows the girl. After we got married, he went back to this girl and I saw Karolina laughing," Savana described ominously.

"Oh mom, it's your mind playing tricks on you. We talked about Karolina all the time and she can be very evil when she wants to. Plus, you know she doesn't want you to be happy. Try not to think too much about her or Dad," Jerry warned. They both said good bye to each other, relieved to hear each other's voice.

"How was Jerry?" asked Gabriele. "He is good and is ready to tackle his school studies," said Savana.

"Now my son really knows his grandmother very well," Savana said.

"Gabriele said that we should leave Karolina alone and just concentrate on our wedding and the restaurant. We have a lot of work to do together!" Now, Savana had her wedding dress and the store where they were going to order the wedding flowers and the decorations.

Gabriele put his arms tenderly around Savana and whispered in her ear: "All the other wedding needs we can purchase in Sicily. My sister and my cousin will be your personal wedding planners," Gabriele said. "We will be flying over to Sicily this weekend. You need to check the wedding venue and express how you want everything to look," said Gabriele with passionate amore.

Chapter Thirty

Gabriele had been observing Savana's menacing melancholy lately. Is Jerry being across the ocean 4000 miles away why you often look sad?" asked Gabriele. "I want you to tell me if you need or want anything. I am glad Jerry has gone back to school so you and I can now find time to talk," said Gabriele.

"I know, we hardly talk. Jerry has occupied my life and now I look forward to true intimacy with you as my husband and best friend, Gabriele" said Savana.

"You need to communicate with me so I know what you need and I know what you don't like and I know when you are upset and sad. I don't want you to try and solve your own problems by yourself. You've asked me if you can do some work in the restaurant. Do what you want to do because very soon you are going to be my wife and co-business owner. I still see the fear in you. Are you afraid of me, Savana?" asked Gabriele.

It took a long time before she answered his questions. "No, I am not afraid of you. I just have to get used to you. I have been hurt by Jasen and it Is taking a long time to get over that."

"I am ready now to really love you, Gabriele," said Savana.

They were both very emotional and they kissed and hugged each other.

Gabriele with tears in his eyes confessed, "I am very happy that you finally told me the truth and we can leave all these bad memories of what these two people Karolina and Jasen have done to you. I know Karolina has been very cruel to you and she treated like you were lower class, but you are very strong person; you fought hard to get over it and you did it."

"You have me. I know fate has brought us together," explained Gabriele.

They hurried to get home because it was getting dark and windy. Savana fixed their dinner of salad and pasta.

Gabriele told Savana, "You look very pretty today." Savana was surprised and smiled. She kissed Gabriele.

"I thought you left already for work," said Savana.

"I will go later today, Gabriele insisted, "I want to make sure you're alright.'When Gabriele came home for dinner, Savana shared a surprise encounter she had that afternoon when she went for a walk in their seaside village. "I met someone who is related to Jasen," said Savana.

"How did you find out?" asked Gabriele.

"Well, I was feeling homesick so I stopped at Starbucks for a cappuccino. When I sat down at the counter, I saw a pretty young American girl sipping her coffee and reading an English fashion magazine. We started up a conversation and soon I realized I had unearthed a blockbuster connection!"

I asked her name and she told me her name is Julia. I asked her if she was brought up here. She told me that she is an American and her mother is Italian. They moved here to attend a relative's wedding after her father died.

"My mother's cousin is ready to marry an Italian woman. She's pregnant," said Julia.

"What is the name of your mother's cousin?" asked Savana. His name is Jasen. His mother and my mom's mother are real sisters.

Her name is Karolina," said Julia.

"When is the wedding?" asked Savana, suppressing her surprise discovery.

"They are not going to have a big wedding. It is going to be a private wedding. They are going to have less than 500 guests and the wedding is going to be in three weeks," said Julia.

This was a big news to Savana and she couldn't wait to tell Gabriele and Jerry. This really was a surprise to meet Karolina's second cousin! Karolina never discussed her relatives at all. She kept them as a secret. Now, Savana uncovered one of her biggest secrets-to actually meet one of her relatives. She was really amazed. They said goodbye and Savana hurried home to tell the news to Gabriele.

Gabriele arrived, and he kissed her and hugged her.

"I met someone today who proved everything we were talking about Jasen and Karolina. Her name is Julia. She happens to be the daughter of Karolina's cousin," explained Savana.

Her American father bought a vineyard and now her Italian mother owns several boutiques here. She then told me a very interesting story. Her cousin's son is getting married in three weeks. His wife to be Sofi is three months pregnant and his name is Jasen. He used to be a doctor in America, but now he owns several vineyards. They want a private wedding and there are only 500 guests invited," said Savana.

"Wow, what a story! Did she ask about you?" asked Gabriele.

"Of course. I did not tell the whole story. I just told her that I am here to get married," said Savana.

"Do you think she is going to tell them that she met you?" Gabriele asked.

"I don't really care and Karolina is going to be asking all the questions," said Savana. "I am just amazed; as much as Karolina wants to keep all the secrets, they will be shouted from the rooftops. Look what happened today," said Savana. "She has a lot of secrets. She knows everyone's life.

"I think I know this cousin of Karolina. She came to America and stayed with Jasen and Karolina. She went to school in some small business schools. She was young like you. Jasen was just starting to be a doctor. He fell in love with her and Karolina found them. She moved out from Karolina's house. Jasen helped her find an apartment. She then met her current husband who happened to be an attorney," explained Gabriele.

"You seem to know all the secrets of Karolina," said Savana."

I already told you that there are more secrets that we are going to discover," said Gabriele.

"Karolina and Jasen invited my parents to the wedding as well. Actually, everyone was invited except us. My father asked me why we were not invited and I told my dad that Karolina never liked you. He then asked me if we are going to invite them to our wedding. I then told him that this invitation was up to you! I told my dad that Karolina always looked at you like you're a poor underling. My dad agreed and he said that's the way they think. They think we are unworthy and financially stretched thin. There is no doubt; they do have a lot of money," said Gabriele.

"I want to tell you something, Gabriele. Karolina's time is coming when all her dirty secrets are going to be thrown at her face. She is very protective of Jasen and all the lies she has been harboring in her dark heart," said Savana. "I am feeling good and very happy. I love you very much, Gabriele. I know I have been distant from you and I am sorry for my behavior. I appreciate everything you are doing for me. Thank you for your love and everything!"

They went to bed and she slept wrapped in his loving arms. That was the first night that Savana really had a good night's sleep. She finally felt rejuvenated and she experienced that her body had been lifted from all the negativity. Her body felt lighter and she was really feeling her true love for Gabriel. She hugged him really tight while they were sleeping.

Chapter
Thirty-One

Julia brought some grapes and invited Savana to a picnic lunch in a grove of olive trees on the mountainside overlooking a steep cliff.

"My mom and I went to see Karolina and I told her about you. She told us that she knew you. My mom asked her how she knew you, and she just said she didn't want to talk about you. My mom is going to see Jasen and she is going to ask him how Karolina knows you," Julia innocently replied.

"Karolina was always different from my mom. She has many secrets. She knows secrets about my mother and even about my dad. My dad couldn't stand Karolina. She always looked down on people. She always thought she was better than anyone else. She did not think that Sofi was good enough for Jasen either, but Jasen told her that she was not going to stop this one. Sofi is carrying his baby and Karolina was not going to mess it up. I overheard her telling my mom that Jasen has a son who is going to school in Harvard. He must be really smart if you go to Harvard. I want to meet him and he is studying business. She won't tell my mom his mother's name," said Julia.

"Maybe one of these days you are going to meet him," Savana told Julia with a wink.

"I want you to tell me about you. I feel that you know more about Karolina and Jasen," Julia said.

"Maybe someday," replied Savana.

"Do you like to go shopping?" asked Julia.

"Yes, I do" replied Savana.

"Great, I will take you to my mom's boutique stores.

"I would love that. Is your mom's boutique down near the ocean?" asked Savana.

"Yes', said Julia.

"I have been there last summer purchasing beautiful necessities for my wedding," said Savana.

"You know, my mom was admiring this guy and his girlfriend and a handsome boy. She said that the boy is very tall and a very good-looking boy and he was with this woman," said Julia.

"I better go home now. My boyfriend is probably home. I will see you tomorrow, Julia." They said good bye until tomorrow.

Savana was very excited she had a lot to tell Gabriele. She called him right away. He answered right away. He asked her if she saw Julia again.

She said "Yes," she shared a picnic lunch with me. She brought some red grapes and they were so sweet I thought I was drinking my favorite Moscato wine. She told Karolina about me, but she just ignored her reports. Very soon they are going to know it was me. I asked Julia if her mother's boutique was down near the ocean and she agreed. She said her mom was telling them one day that she saw a handsome guy with a very pretty woman and a very tall good-looking boy own at ocean and she hoped they would come again," Savana said to Gabriele.

"Are you going to tell her who those people were?" asked Gabriele.

"Yes, I am going to tell her. She wants us to go and see her mother's boutique. I think we are going to be very good friends. I feel that I've found my lost sister. She said things that I already knew," said Savana. "Is it okay with you if I invite her to come over and visit?" asked Savana.

"Yes, you can invite her to come over," answered Gabriele. "How old is Julia?"

"She is two years younger than me. We are just about in the same age group," said Savana.

Just then Gabriel's father Bruno called from Sicily. Gabriel told his father that he had met the girl of his dreams.

"Well, it was all meant to be. You have been looking for a wife and now you finally met her."

"Yes, Dad, I really like Savana. She is very humble and respectful and ,of course, beautiful."

Do you know what her parents do?" he asked Gabriele.

"Both of her parents are attorneys and her brother is going to graduate from law school and her youngest brother is still in college," Gabriele said.

"Looks like she comes from a decent and well-educated family," said his father.

"Very soon we are going to meet them in person. They are all looking forward to attending the wedding. I haven't talked to them yet, but I will be talking to them when we are visiting Sicily next week," said Gabriele.

"Jerry is going to be like his grandparents and I am very proud of you son for your patience, courage, and kindness. Look at you, your business is booming and very soon Savana will be helping you," said his father.

"I'm very happy with Savana, dad. She is very unique and kind and humble. That's what make her very special," said Gabriele.

Gabriele was excited and looked forward to meeting Savana's parents.

"The Sicilians are all about amore," Gabriele boasted. They are very loving and friendly.

"Savana's parents have known that and they feel very blessed that Savana found someone who loves her very much compared to Karolina and Jasen. Karolina is controlling Jasen and it is sad to see a grown old man who cannot make his own decisions. As Karolina rules, it is all about money and power. Karolina believes that she is a very high-class woman. Her mother was the king of Italy's sister and that's why she treated Savana with contempt. Savana comes from a nice family who love Savana very much. As a matter of fact, they want her to come back because of the way Jasen and his mother have treated her. She told them that she has now met a very loving man and she loves him very much. She is looking forward to marrying me and believes that her life will be completed," Gabriele proudly shared with his father,

Chapter
Thirty-Two

"Julia, tell me more about Jasen's wedding," Savana asked, eager for more news.

"They said it was going to be a private affair, but many relatives are coming from Europe and America. I think they are all cousins of Jasen," said Julia. She asked Savana again if she wanted to come to the wedding with her. Savana just thanked her and turned down the invitation.

Gabriele was still at the restaurant and Savana decided to go and see him. Gabriele noticed her right away.

"This is a nice surprise that you come and see me here," said Gabriele to Savana.

"I really missed you today and I decided to surprise you," Savana said. "I was with Julia sharing local news."

"I am glad to hear that. Every day you are meeting new friends and I am happy for you Savana," said Gabriele.

"I am glad too. It makes me happy when I communicate with different people and that's how I know what kind of people they are," Savana replied. "Julia invited me again to Jasen's wedding which is next week as they try to keep it as a secret. Karolina cannot hide her secrets anymore. She wants to keep this one with a tight lid but someone else knows her secret," said Savana.

"Oh really! I know, my dad and mom are invited and I haven't spoken with either one of them," said Gabriele. "Have you talked to Jerry?" asked Gabriele.

"I will call him tonight," said Savana. "Speaking of the devil, he is calling me now!"

"Mom, do you know that dad is getting married next week?" asked Jerry. "I know because some girl from school told me. "Did they invite you?" asked Jerry.

"No" said Savana. "Why are you asking me this question when you already know the answer, Jerry," scolded his mother.

"I just need to know, if we are still part of dad's family," said Jerry.

"Your grandma has turned her eyes away from us. She should invite you as well because this baby will be your sibling. He is going to be a father soon. He has to take care of two children. Let's not think or worry about them. You study hard so you can graduate and find a good job," said Savana, with a strong sense of the American independence and work ethic.

"I am doing very well in school mom. I want to take law next. I have not mentioned it to dad yet. I want to surprise him."

"Yesterday, I went and surprised Gabriel at the restaurant. He was very happy that I surprised him. He was worrying about me that I did not confide in him and tell him what I need and how I feel."

"I was worrying about you too, mom. I felt that you were unhappy and lonely. I think about you all the time, but now I can see you are happy and that makes me very happy too, mom," said Jerry lovingly.

"Gabriele and I are going to Sicily next week. We have to prepare for the wedding. He decided that we should get married on the boat. His mother said that we should have a church wedding but have our honeymoon on the yacht."

"He's going to think about it," said Savana.

"I hope he is going to make the right decision and that he is going to make you happy mom. I better go to bed. I have a big test tomorrow on family law," said Jerry.

Savana was very happy that she talked to her son. 'What did Jerry have to say?" asked Gabriele.

"He asked me I if knew that his father was getting married next week," she told Gabriele.

"I think he has been talking with his father and Karolina is the one who is running the show and she does not like you. It is really sad that she is looking at you like that, but all we can do is wish them good luck," said Gabriele. "We will be in Sicily during their wedding. My dad called me today, and told me that they are attending Jasen's wedding. I told him that we're coming to Sicily to prepare for our wedding celebration. I told my dad that your parents are coming to visit Sicily. I think your brothers will also be joining them. "

My father is looking forward to meeting them, too," said Gabriele.

"I am very happy that my parents are coming to visit us. They have heard about Sicily a lot and have seen alluring pictures of the Island. They have some friends that have been to Sicily and now they are really coming to Sicily," said Savana.

"I am excited to meet them too," said Gabriele.

Chapter Thirty-Three

Gabriele got up early and fixed their breakfast before Savana woke up feeling a bit blah and sad. They said goodbye and he left for work. Savana was alone in the house, but she was looking forward to her parents' arrival the next month. She suddenly remembered that Julia wanted to meet her for coffee at 10 am. They greeted each other and Julia had some news to share with Savana.

"I heard today that you are the mother of Jasen's son!" she said to Savana. "Who said that to you?" asked Savana.

"My mom was talking to Karolina and she said that Jasen has a son named Jerry who is going to college in America and my mom asked her who was his mother. She mentioned your name," she told Savana.

"I want to meet this Savana. I want to talk to her," my mother said to Karolina. "Why did Jasen not marry her?" she asked her.

"I did not want Jasen to marry her because she was not good enough for Jasen," she told my mother. "My mom was very upset and left her alone in their house."

"Please, will you come with me to meet my mom?" begged Julia.

"Okay, I will come with you."

She thanked Savana. Julia called her mother and told her the news. Her mother was very happy. She asked Julia to come with her to the restaurant to tell Gabriele. Gabriele was happy to see both of them.

"I am glad to meet you, Julia. Savana talks about you all the time," he spoke.

"Her mother has a boutique not very far away from here. I will see you at home later," Savana informed Gabriele.

"OK, have a nice time," said Gabriele.

Julia's mother was very happy to meet Savana.

"Oh! What a lovely person you are. My daughter came and told me about you the first time and I was glad that she met someone as nice as you. She talks about you every day. I've heard everything about you and Jasen. I really felt upset that he did not want to marry you and you had a handsome son with him who is going to school in America now. He is staying with you. Jasen is also my cousin, Karolina's son. I know, that she did not treat you well. She didn't want Jasen to marry you. How evil is that? She has a lot of secrets she has not told anyone. Her brother knows a lot of secrets too and he told his sister Karolina every secret that he knew. I heard that you are getting married in December!" exclaimed Julia's mother.

"Yes, I am. We decided to get married in December when Jerry is done with school. My parents and relatives are coming also. It's going to be a great wedding and we are going to have our honeymoon in the yacht," said Savana with great expectation.

"Are you going to invite Jasen and his new wife?"

"I don't think that we are going to invite them."

"I just want to tell you something, dear Savana: "Karolina is evil and has a lot of evil secrets. I am glad that Jasen is finally getting married and having a new baby. He is been listening to his mother for a long time and finally, she approved a wife for him."

Slightly changing the subject, Julia's mother asked Savanna: "How old is Jerry?"

"He is eighteen years old and he is going to one of the best schools in America because he is a very smart boy," she proudly answered.

"It is very sad that she did not accept you and her grandson as well. "

Savana then confided. "I hate to tell you this, but Jerry does not like his grandmother. Like you, he calls Karolina an evil woman. He especially did not like her when he found out that she told Jasen not to marry me because I was not good enough. He's going to confront Karolina when he sees her. I am glad that Jasen found a wife because he needed that. If he kept listening to Karolina, he would never find a wife," said Savana.

"She is a selfish old lady for not inviting you to Jasen's wedding," said Julia's mother.

"I always feel sad for Jasen for how she's treating him. She thinks that Jasen is a little boy and she treats him like a child. She is also super protective of him. And she is threatening him because of the money and power she has," said Savana.

"He should leave her because he has his own money. I just don't understand. He needs to leave her alone and move on," said Julia's mom.

Chapter
Thirty-Four

"I must go home now; Gabriele is probably waiting for me at home," said Savana. They said good bye and left for home. Gabriele was already waiting for her.

"How was your visit with Julia's mom, Savana?' asked Gabriele.

"I really enjoyed it. She is very different from her cousin Karolina and she is not stuck up like Karolina. She is very pleasant and nice," said Savana.

"Let's have our dinner," suggested Gabriele. "There is one thing I want to tell you. We should not associate ourselves with Karolina and Jasen anymore. We should take care of our own business since we have a lot to do and you need to concentrate on our wedding plans. Karolina was trying to make you jealous. She wants you to go and talk with Jasen and tell him that you still love him. She is really a devil!" Gabriele said with a fierce conviction.

Savana stated with a strong pledge: "I will stay away from both of them. But she will not be able to stop Jerry from speaking with his dad!"

"I know you are getting tired of hearing about these two people. This is what Karolina wants. She is causing all this confusion so you leave me and go back to America. She doesn't want you to be happy," said Gabriele.

Savana added an accurate description of her son's strengths: "Karolina figured already that Jerry is going to be a big problem for her and Jasen. He is very smart; he knows how to talk, and he can tell them both off. He is not afraid to say whatever he wants."

"Karolina is a very smart lady. She knows how to control her son and how to manipulate him. Unfortunately, Jason is very loyal to his mother. I think Jasen purposely made Sofi pregnant to escape his mother's power over him. He is getting tired of his mother's bossy ways," concluded Gabriele.

Gabriele was tired and he told Savana that he was going to sleep. Savana stayed up for a while before she joined Gabriele. They both got up early in the morning and he told Savana he had to leave because they had a very busy day. He kissed her and he left for work. Savana got dressed and left for school. Julia saw her, and she walked over to her and wished a good morning to her.

"My mom really likes you Savana. She wished that you and Jasen could have been married. You are well matched," Julia reiterated her mother's opinion.

"I want to tell you something very important, Julia. My husband to be, Gabriele, doesn't want me to discuss Karolina and Jasen any more. I can't leave them alone. He told to me not to get involved with them at all. My son Jerry is always talking to his father and we can't stop that. Jerry is very outspoken and he can very easily set them straight," said Savana.

"I am sorry Savana. We'll just have to leave them alone." Julia had to leave right away to get ready for Jasen and Sofi's wedding.

Savana then decided to visit the school library where she suddenly discovered a book in the library which was called *Secrets of Italy*. She was very excited to take it home and read it. She wanted to show Gabriele too. She went home and started to read it. There was one story in the book that caught her eye. It was Karolina's family name. These were the secrets that Karolina had been keeping from anyone who knew her.

These family secrets dated back to when her great grandfather was alive. His name was Roberto. He was very wealthy and he had three wives. The first wife was from Spain and he had one son with her, then he left her and married a woman from France who had no children with him and then he left her to marry a third wife who was an Italian woman and he sired three children with her. One of them was Karolina's great grandfather. He contracted some rare disease and they put him away in a hospital which they kept secret from the extended family. Nobody went to visit him because they did not know the location of the hospital. The family was debating if the hospital even really existed.

Karolina's father was named after this sick great grandfather. Karolina did not want to tell this secret to anyone because it would bring embarrassment to her fake social projection of perfection. She decided to keep it as a secret. Savana now knew one of Karolina's secrets, but she knew there must be other genetic hidden family facts so she continued to read the book.

Gabriele arrived and he noticed Savana was already home.

"What are you doing?" he asked her.

"Oh! You are home!" she said. Savana was happy to see Gabriele was home. She needed to share these disturbing stories. "I decided to go to the library to read some books and I found this very interesting book. The title is called *The Secrets of Italy* and I was curious when I saw it."

"And what did you find out?" asked Gabriele.

"I found a big secret that Karolina has been hiding," said Savana.

"What did I tell you?" said Gabriele with a frown on his face.

"I know you already told me to stay away from Karolina and I am sorry that I found this, but I did not know that her family was going to be in there," said Savana.

"I already told you the story that she came from a very wealthy family. Her great grandfather had a lot of money," said Gabriele.

"But you missed out something. Her grandfather caught a strange disease and they took him and admitted him in some hospital far away from the family," Savana relayed with an air of sleuthing. "I questioned myself: Was he really sick or did they just get rid of him so that they could confiscate his money?" Savana asked wondering.

"I never heard that story, but all I know is that her great grandfather had a lot of money and he had several wives," replied Gabriele.

In an attempt to steer the conversation away from Karolina, Gabriele commented: "Jasen is getting married today. They ordered some food from us. Some real Italian food and some Sicilian food also. I know they've contacted my dad and asked if he could bring some Sicilian wine as well," said Gabriele.

"Julia told me yesterday that their relatives from Spain are going to be in the wedding and their relatives from France are going to be there too. As you can see, their aristocratic relatives go back to the 17th century. Her great grandfather married a Spanish woman," said Gabriele.

"Yes, I know, I read it in the book," said Savana.

"He had only one son with her. But this son had six children. He had four sons and two daughters. They all grew up to be very wealthy. There were secrets about the two daughters too. One eloped with the prince of Spain and they didn't have any children and the second daughter was married to a very wealthy Italian who owned several vineyards and she eloped with a German and nobody knew what happened to her," said Gabriele.

"You seem to know their history very well," said Savana.

"Well, my great grandfather used to be very good friends with them and they used to tell each other some very old stories. That's why Karolina knows many secrets and some of them she couldn't tell because the stories were sad but most of them, she is not afraid to tell," explained Gabriele.

"I knew, right away, that she was very secretive when I first met her," said Savana confidently.

"We'll just wait and see what kind of secret she is going to tell now," said Gabriele.

"Have you heard anything about Jasen's wedding?" asked Savana.

"I am waiting for my parents to call me any time now to tell me all about it," replied Gabriele.

Chapter
Thirty-Six

"We just cannot stop talking about Karolina because her life is fascinating to us," said Savana.

"I should agree with what you said about her. Gabriele repeated his opinion of Karolina: "She is a tough woman who is very controlling. You witness what she did to Jasen. She wanted only the best for her son. We both knew that. I think she made a mistake when she didn't want you to marry Jasen. Look at Jerry, how smart he is. I am sure Jasen has mentioned him so many times to his mother and now, she is regretting it," said Gabriele.

"My dad is calling now, let's hear what he has to say about the wedding," exclaimed Gabriele.

"Hi dad, how are you? And how was the wedding?" Gabriele asked Bruno his father.

"The wedding was very nice and they invited five hundred people. Sofi is seven months pregnant. The rumor has been going around that she was three months pregnant. Karolina tried to keep it as a secret but someone revealed the truth. She was very upset that this truth came out. I asked her why she did not invite you and

Savana. She said that you are both very busy. I know she does not like Savana. I saw Jasen, but he didn't look very happy. I went and talked to him for a while. I told him how Jerry is a very smart young man. Jasen agreed and said, my son loves his mother and will do anything for her."

"I also told Jasen, said Bruno, that Savana's parents are coming to visit Sicily for Gabriele's and Savana's Christmas wedding. And we're looking forward to meeting them," Bruno said with genuine Sicilian warmth.

"Also, we learned at the wedding" Bruno confided, that Jasen and Sofia are not going for their honeymoon because of Sofi's pregnancy. They decided to stay in Italy until Sofi has the baby. Karolina was very quiet during the elaborate reception and did not talk to anyone.

Julia spoke to her mother and asked her about her aunt Karolina's strange silence. Her mother explained to her another secret - that there is something wrong with Sofia's baby. Her mother did not ask any more questions.

"I want to talk about the wedding," Savana exclaimed in a hushed tone.

"Well, it was a nice wedding with about five hundred guests. There were a lot of enticing foods. We had some Sicilian and American and Spanish and French dishes that were absolutely scrumptious and acknowledged the married couple's rich heritage. Karolina was strangely quiet throughout the night. My mom just told me that Karolina told her about her secret. There is something wrong with Sofia's baby."

Chapter Thirty-Seven

"She's almost eight months pregnant," said Julia.

"What! I thought she is three months pregnant." replied Savana in shock.

"I heard that too. You know Karolina has to be very secretive of everything," said Julia.

"Are they going somewhere for their honeymoon?" asked Savana.

"No, they are not going anywhere because of Sofia's pregnancy. They are afraid she is going to lose the baby," said Julia sadly.

"My mom wants you to stop by Savana's house. She has a gift for you. I told her that your parents are coming to visit and you are going to Sicily this week," said Julia.

"I would love to stop by, Julia. I like your mom. She is very different from her cousin. Let me call Gabriele and ask him.

Savana called Gabriele right away and he told her: "I will pick you up from there. I want to meet Julia's mother too!" They went to see Julia's mother's boutique. She was glad to see Savana.

"Julia told me that you are going to Sicily," responded Julia's mom.

"Yes, I am looking forward to going and I am even more excited that my parents are going to meet us there. We want to prepare too for our wedding," said Savana.

"I am very happy for you and Gabriele," emoted Julia's mom, Isabella. "I am sure Julia has told you about the wedding. It was a pretty wedding. A lot of food and wine. We had Sicilian foods and American foods. I was thinking about you. Well, they have known each other for a very long time. Karolina was supposed to marry Gabriele's father Bruno, but she married someone else," Julia's mother explained.

"I am wishing them good wishes and I pray the baby is going to be okay," said Savana.

Julia's mother gave her presents and she also included presents for her parents. Savana was very happy and thankful to Julia's mom. Savana told her that Gabriele is stopping by and he would like to meet you, Isabella.

"I am looking forward to meeting him too," said Isabella. "When is Jerry coming home?" she asked Savana.

"He is coming in December," replied Savana. "I am looking forward to seeing him. My cousin said that he is a very good-looking boy and tall. He looks like his father and is very smart. My cousin Karolina also said that Jerry was the epitome of chivalry, always protecting his mom."

"What is chivalry?" Savana asked.

Her cousin replied that it was a Christian code of conduct for medieval knights.

Gabriele surprised them. Isabella, Julia's mom, was very happy to meet him for the first time. "Your parents were at the wedding last night and we had Sicilian foods and American dishes. It was a nice wedding. Sofia is seven months pregnant and they just found out that something is wrong with the baby and they are not going anywhere for their honeymoon. Karolina has been very quiet about Sofi's pregnancy but I think there is more to it," said Isabella.

"That is very sad to hear. I just want to wish them well," said Gabriele. "We are going home now." They all said good bye to each other.

Savana went home and Gabriele told Savana to start packing up her clothes to get ready to leave the next day.

They both packed up all their things and went to bed early that night. The cab arrived at 7 am. They got to the airport, checked in all their suitcases, and went straight to the boarding place. Their flight was scheduled to leave at 10 am. They boarded the plane and arrived in Sicily only two hours later at high noon. Sicily boasts beautiful land and seascapes. Inns that are perched on cliffs with wooden decks hanging at all angles -perfect for watching the ocean sneak into little stony bays that harbor brightly colored fishing boats. This image is created especially for postcards and tourists who enjoy the Mediterranean sea climate.

Gabriele's father met them at the airport and he was very happy to see them.

"Are you excited to see your parents, Savana?" asked Bruno.

"Yes, I am happy to see them. I know, they have been wanting to visit Sicily for a very long time. Little did they know that their daughter would marry a Sicilian!" said Savana and the three of them laughed really hard.

"We are really looking forward to meeting them too," said Gabriele. "The history of Sicily is very interesting and I am sure, both of them as lawyers must know the history of the island," said Bruno.

"Yes, my parents know about the history of the islands and some of their friends have been here and told them how beautiful the island is and they have often encouraged them to come and see first hand!"

"How appropriate that they have chosen to come at this time," said Bruno.

Gabriele owned a big five-bedroom villa near the ocean. He hired many workers to prepare his house for Savana's parents' arrival that weekend.

Chapter Thirty-Eight

They went back to the house and Gabriele's father Bruno was waiting outside. He went inside the house with them and told them his mother was inviting them to come have dinner with them. Other relatives were going to be there as well and they all wanted to meet Savana. He told his father that he was going to take Savana to Tunisia next week. Bruno replied that it was a very good idea because it was a beautiful country that was close by.

They went to dinner at Bruno's house and most of the relatives were there. They all liked Savana and they all knew that Gabriele was marrying her. Two of Gabriele's cousins were lawyers and Gabriel's younger brother as well. Gabriele introduced all of them to Savana who was a bit overwhelmed and found it difficult to pronounce and remember their Sicilian names. She knew Gabriele's younger brother's name was Mario. His cousins' names were Roberto, Giovanni and Antonio. Gabriele had one sister whose name was Serafina and they had two women cousins named Paola and Valentina. Gabriele also had one uncle named Roberto and his mother's name was Livia.

Savana tried to remember all the names because she knew all these relative's names would be important after she married Gabriele. She had a chance to talk to Gabriele's brother, Marco.

"Are you excited about you parents coming to Sicily?" he asked Savana.

"I am very excited. I haven't seen them for two years now!" she joyfully exclaimed.

"My brother told me that your parents are both lawyers."

"Yes, they are," said Savana. My father is well known for successfully prosecuting criminals throughout California."

"I am also an Attorney here in Sicily and I am very busy," he told Savana. "I am very happy for you and my brother and I am certain that he made the right decision to marry you. He has been looking for a wife for quite a long time now until he saw you at his restaurant when you were celebrating your birthday. He immediately fell in love with you, Savana. He was told you were with Jasen and also that you had a son with him. When he heard that Jasen rejected marrying you, he felt really bad and he was determined to talk to you," Marco explained to Savana.

"I will never forget how he helped me and I owe him my whole life. He is very loving, kind and understanding. I am very thankful to God for answering my prayer. Jerry, my son is very happy with Gabriele also," said Savana.

"I am very proud of you for standing strong and believing the truth. I want to congratulate you for marrying my brother," Marco said.

"Are you going to settle down soon like Gabriele?" Savana asked him.

"I haven't found one girl yet but I am dating and looking as well! And believe me, you will be the first one to know," he said. "I am very busy in Sicily prosecuting criminals. We have crimes that are very complicated. We have some cold cases that I am working on right now. There was a dispute with families and crimes committed. Families fighting among themselves concerning old money that was brought down from their previous great grandfather. Some families accused each other and a lot of fighting ensued and it cannot be resolved. Many of them are very wealthy," Marco recounted.

"I know, Karolina has many secrets but there is one very important secret that she has not told. I heard how she mistreated you and I truly believe that she is afraid you will know the secret."

"They are very wealthy and she didn't want Jasen to marry anyone but a wealthy Italian woman. You see, the woman that Jasen married is on the same step of the social ladder with Karolina. Her parents have old money. I heard Sofi is having a problem with her baby. I heard Karolina has been very upset about it."

"I hate to tell you this, but she deserves all these cruel happenings because of how badly she treats people," Savana said.

The family was very happy with Savana and felt that she fit right in with their family. Gabriele and Savana said "Grazia arrivederci" to his family and went home to soundly sleep. They were looking forward for her parents to arrive the next day.

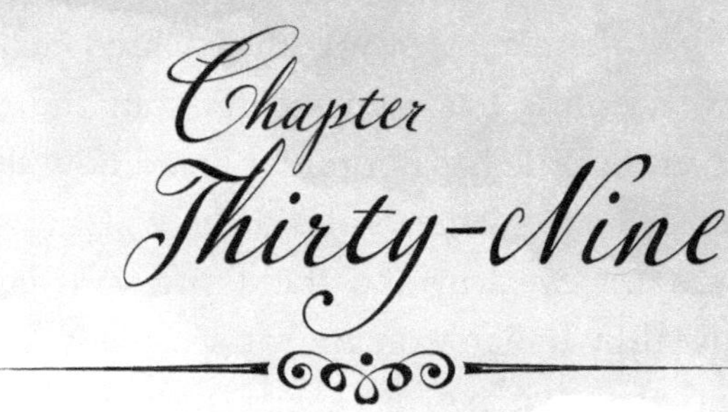

Chapter Thirty-Nine

They both went to the airport to wait for her parents' arrival. Finally, the big moment had arrived. Savana rushed to meet her parents with tears of happiness. It had been over two years since she had seen her family.

"You look good Savana," her mother said.

"You both look great mother and dad!" Savana replied.

She introduced Gabriele to her parents. They liked him and were very happy for their daughter for choosing Gabriele. They drove to their hotel and got situated. They took them to Gabriele's restaurant. They admired the Mediterranean ocean and the weather. They enjoyed their pasta and salad. Gabriele invited them for dinner to meet his family.

"Our friends have been here so many times and they always tell us to come and visit Sicily. It is the most beautiful island in the world. The people are friendly and the food is to die for. We are very happy that you're marrying our daughter," Savana's parents said to Gabriele. At one point when she was mistreated by Jasen and his mother, we asked Savana to come back home.

"Karolina has many secrets but she has one that she herself is scared to reveal," said Mark.

Her parents went back to their hotel and got ready for dinner. They talked about their daughter how lucky she was to meet Gabriele It looked like he came from a very good family. They looked forward to meeting Gabriele's family during dinner. The Mediterranean weather was very good. The evening breeze was lovely. Gabriele's restaurant was beautiful. Savana introduced her parents to Gabriele's family. They all were happy to meet each other. They talked about the beauty, history, and charm of Sicily They had been wanting to come and visit the island, but their work had been delaying them.

"When Savana told us they were moving to Italy with Jasen and his mother, we were very happy. I asked if he was going to marry her and she said not right away. He asked her to take care of Jerry. He was only three years old. Savana always stayed connected with us. The time came when she told us that she was not happy and Karolina mistreated her. Jasen told her that they were not going to get married. They were living together. She just couldn't stay with them any longer. Jerry was going to school during that time. They decided to go and celebrate Savana's birthday at Gabriele's restaurant. And you know the rest of the story. We are very thankful to you," recounted Savana's mother.

"My father Bruno told me the story about the beauty of Savana and how Jasen wouldn't marry her. I had been looking for a wife for a while when she walked into my restaurant that night. I fell in love with her right away when I saw her. It was like a dream. Here we are! I am ready to marry her," said Gabriele.

"I am glad that Savana will be married into a good family," her father said unsuspecting of any hidden barriers.

Chapter Forty

"I am planning to take you all to visit Tunisia which is right across from us in Sicily. We can fly or take the boat. They speak Arabic and it is a Muslim country. It is a very beautiful country. Savana has not been there yet either," said Gabriele. They decided to go and visit Tunisia on the next day. The next morning, they prepared themselves to leave. Gabriele decided to take his car to Tunisia. His parents and his two brothers were coming too. He had a very big SUV that held ten people. They took the boat across until they got to Tunisia.

The beaches were pretty. They just loved the weather. They toured the city and decided to get out from the vehicle and walk on the beach. There were many people on the beach even though it was cool during the day. Gabriele had been in Tunisia before. He was there to see how they cooked their foods and to taste the different kind of spices for his restaurant. The Tunisia main dish always included couscous, small steamed granules of semolina. He took Savana's parents to a famous Tunisia restaurant. He wanted them to taste how different the North African food was from Italian food which is the reason why Sicilian food tasted so different. The history and ethnicity of Sicily was a mix of other races including African.

Savana's parents really enjoyed the foods the ocean and the people. They were very happy that their daughter had found a wonderful and loving man to marry. It was getting late and it was time for them to get back home. The boat ride was lovely. They enjoyed the cool breeze and the beautiful bright lights behind them as their boat left Tunisia for Sicily. They were very tired and wanted to get to their hotel so they could say good night to Savana and Gabriele. They only had two more days before they returned to America.

Bruno had asked them to join them for a winery tour the next day. The tour was beautiful and Bruno told them about how Karolina's parents were very wealthy. They were going to buy his vineyard, but they changed their mind and then Jasen came along and decided to buy a vineyard. He was like his grandfather. He did exactly the same thing. Jasen did not tell the whole story, so I told Savana about it. Savana was still living with them at that time.

"Karolina's father was involved with bad money. They had many secrets and Karolina didn't want to tell anyone. I've known their family for a very long time. As a matter of fact, Karolina and I were supposed to get married but she married someone else. I think, she was afraid that I was going to know all their secrets. Karolina was always secretive. She was the one who caused Jasen not to marry Savana. She said that Savana was not good enough for her son," Bruno spoke. "I remember when little Jerry was born, I went to visit them. I noticed Jasen was very happy and very much in love with Savana. I met Karolina and she was not very happy when she saw me. I knew it back then that she was not happy with Savana.

"We are very happy that our daughter Savana has met a handsome man and a very loving man," said Savana's mother. Both families were looking forward to Savana and Gabriele's wedding.

Savana's parents were getting ready to return to America. They had time alone with Savana. "We noticed that Gabriele is still attached to Karolina. We want you to be very careful. There is something I noticed that I still can't put together.

Has Gabriele had a relationship before?" asked Savana's father.

"I don't really know dad. I am just beginning to know him. He is very honest with me and is always worrying about me."

"I am worried about you because it looks like Karolina controls them too," Savana's father shared.

Savana responded saying "I am not even worried about Karolina. I heard she is getting sick all the time and Sofi's pregnancy is not going very well. I heard Sofi is going to lose the baby and she was not talking or saying anything at all throughout the marriage celebration. I have not spoken to her since I left them but I have spoken to Jasen. Jerry and I went to have lunch with him and he did not look happy at all. Karolina deserves her problems for all the cruel things she has done to people. She treated me like dirt and she did not want me to marry her son. Jasen and I were really in love until she ruined it. Jerry just hates her after he knew how she had been treating me."

I don't know if Jasen has been talking because you can see the pain inside his eyes. Money is more important to him than me. Jasen has been missing Jerry. He is just like his dad. Jasen really wants him to run the business when he gets out from school. Jerry has a big surprise for him. He wants to study law and the school has told him that he can take them both. Jerry is going to be done next year and he should be done next fall with his law," Savana told her parents.

"Jerry is a very smart boy!" Savana's father said.

"Do you know why he wanted to be a lawyer?" asked Savana. "To prosecute Karolina!"

His father and mother burst out laughing." Really!" said her mother.

"I told Jerry how Karolina had been treating me and he saw it himself. He told me to move out from them and find another place," said Savana.

They were impressed about Jerry. He is very smart.

"The lawyer side comes from us. Look how many lawyers are in our family!" said her father.

"We will see him on the wedding day," said her mother.

"I miss my son. He always comforts me and he always asks me to go for a walk with him," said Savana. " I remember Jasen told me once that Jerry is smart like him, but his ways of dealing with people are more like his mom. He is very outspoken and he likes to know the truth." said Savana. "He will fit in very well in Sicily to prosecute those mobs. Bruno told us one day that Karolina's father was in the mob and that is one of her biggest secrets and she can't tell it to anybody.

"I seriously think that she is afraid of you, Savana," her father told her.

"I felt that too and she is afraid that I will know something that she has been hiding for a very long time. I found it very strange that for the longest time she did not want any woman to get closer to Jasen."

Chapter Forty-One

We went to Hawaii one time and I saw him packing his clothes and hers in one suitcase. I told him not to do it. She was going to pack her clothes in my suitcase because we are both women. He left her clothes alone and when we got to our hotel, we unpacked everything and put both of their suitcases in the bedroom. I saw that they were sleeping together in the bedroom in one bed. I stood up and asked Jasen why were they sleeping together on the same bed. I told her that she needed to come and sleep with me because we are both women or let her sleep in one bed and I sleep on the other bed. And Jasen could come and sleep in the living room!" said Savana. "They were behaving like lovers. They would be feeding each other like a new husband and new wife."

"I found it very strange. She hated me when she found out I was pregnant. She has been holding her own son for herself. I am glad that Jasen married Sofi. Jasen is getting old and he needs someone to take care of him. He is very proud of Jerry. We were going to have another baby but we decided to wait until we got here. Things changed really fast. His mother made me very miserable so I decided to leave and it was the luckiest day of my life, not only did I move out from that house but the most important part, I found the love of life!" said Savana to her parents.

"We love you very much and we are very proud of you as well," said her parents earnestly.

We talked about you all the time and that's why we asked so many times, to come back home but you held on and you are very strong, Savana, and you know how to overcome all those ridiculous problems. I am glad that you do not talk to Karolina. It is better she leaves you alone," said her mother. "I heard that she has been missing Jerry and she wanted Jerry to come and visit her. Jerry goes to visit his father all the time and she always shows up to see Jerry. "

"He is good looking and very tall and he looks more like Jasen now that he's older."

"I am going to really miss both of you, but not for long because you are going to be back here soon," said Savana.

"That's right, we must come back and see you and Gabriele get married," said her father.

They said goodbye the next day. They all went to the airport. Savana's parent said goodbye to both of them and said they were looking forward to seeing them for the wedding. Savana and Gabriele flew back to Italy. Savana missed her parents already. Gabriele and Savana both looked tired and exhausted. They both went straight to bed.

Gabriele got up in the morning and left for work while Savana slept on. She was awakened with a phone call. It was her son Jerry. "Hi mom! Are you still sleeping?" asked Jerry.

"Oh! Jerry, how are you, my son? We just got back from Sicily yesterday. Grandma and your grandpa came from America to visit," said Savana.

"I forgot all about that. Did they enjoy their visit?" asked Jerry.

"Very much so. Gabriele took us to see Tunisia. What a wonderful country with a rich history going back to the Roman

Empire and Phoenicia. Gabriele brought many couscous recipes back to his restaurants. And my parents really enjoyed their short boat trip to the Northern African coast of Tunisia.

"Also, Jerry, Savana continued sharing the latest news with her son, your dad got married to Sofi and you probably already know, she is four months pregnant. Sofi is having some kind of problem with the pregnancy and she is very sick. Karolina has been very quiet lately. I heard that she is not happy with Sofi at all." Said Savana.

"She deserves all this bad karma because she is evil and who knows she probably did something to Sofi not to have the baby," said Jerry.

That is not very nice Jerry," scolded his mother, although she agreed with his sentiment.

"She did not invite you to dad's wedding and she has been very secretive about it, but she cannot hide it anymore. Sofia is pregnant and the baby who is my half-sister is sick," said Jerry.

"I am going to ask Gabriele if we can go to Tunisia before the wedding," said Savana.

"Yes!" Jerry said excitedly. "We still have a lot of time before the wedding day. Can we go by ourselves because Gabriele is going to be busy?" asked Jerry.

"I don't think Gabriele is going to allow us to go by ourselves. It is a Muslim country and they speak Arabic," said Savana.

"Mom, we have to stop relying on him. We need to do things by ourselves. I learn a lot that way."

"That's true but I was scared to see the people myself and I really wondered about all the women who wear the Muslim veil and long dress. Who are they really? I am used to understanding people partially by their physical appearance. Every time I passed this one masked woman who seemed to be following us, she always gave me these looks that made me feel uncomfortable."

"Mom, you sound paranoid. I don't want you to be scared of people. They are probably thinking scary thoughts about you too!" Jerry said laughing to lighten the mood.

Chapter Forty-Two

Savana collected all her books and her bag and left the house. Julia was already waiting for her. They hugged each other and sat down on the bench.

"Missed you Savana! How was your trip?" asked Julia.

"I really had a very nice time. I had to spend time with my parents. I haven't seen them for two years. We went to Tunisia and what a pretty country! We went to the beach and it was beautiful. We ate some delicious exotic Tunisian food. My parents loved the side trip to Tunisia and they are so excited to come back to this part of the world for the wedding in December," Savana said with pure joy.

"I am glad you had a nice time. I didn't do very much but I helped my mother at her boutique. I have some sad news to tell you about Jasen and Sofia. She is going to lose the baby. The baby has some kind of illness. If she is going to keep the baby, she is going to lose her own life. Jasen is taking it very hard. My mom talked to him and told him that they could have another baby. It is not the end of the world. Sofia still is very young. Karolina has not said anything at all. I heard that she was not happy with Sofia at all. She even made a comment that It would be good for Sofia to lose the baby as far as her health is concerned," said Julia.

"She wants Jasen to herself," said Savana.

"That's what mom said," said Julia.

"She is very evil and selfish. I hope her time of reckoning is coming soon," said Savana vindictively.

"She knew that you are getting married in December. She made a comment about your son. She hasn't seen him for a long time. She hopes that you will be inviting her to your wedding only so she can see Jerry," Julia compassionately confided.

"She has some guts to say that. We are not going to invite her, but Jerry can go visit her and that's all," said Savana.

"I heard some strange news," Julia continued. My mom and I were at Karolina's house over the weekend. Her phone rang and a man was on the phone. She went downstairs to take the call and she didn't hang up the one in the living room. We could hear everything. She was asking the man on the phone how was their trip to Tunisia. The man's voice was old. She was asking about you. He said that you were very happy and she asked about your parents. The man said that he was very surprised that they were both lawyers. Karolina responded, yes, Savana comes from a very good family, but she was not good enough to marry my son. It could have been Gabriele's father. You can ask him," Julia said.

Savana commented: "That is very strange if Bruno, my future father-in-law, was talking about me to Karolina."

"I am going to have my mom tell you the story about Gabriele's family and Karolina's family," said Julia. As a matter of fact, Bruno and Karolina were supposed to get married but she went and married someone else and that's why her life is so messed up and confusing. Does Bruno like you?" asked Julia.

"That's a very good question. I've met him several times before but I have not made conversation. I always wonder if he really likes me or not," said Savana.

"I just hope he and Karolina are not plotting something bad," said Julia suspiciously.

I hope not," said Savana. "I will bet Gabriele knows about this. I found Gabriele always acting very strange after he speaks with his father all the time. I want to tell you something that's very odd that happened while we were in Tunisia. While I was talking with my parents on the beach, Gabriele disappeared for a while and I was looking for him. In the distance, I saw him talking to a woman and I saw his father Bruno joining them. He saw me looking for him and he rushed over to us. I did not say anything to him," said Savana.

"You really need to talk to my mother. She knows a lot of stories," said Julia.

"Can we go and see her now?" asked Savana.

"Yes, of course. Are you going to tell Gabriele?" asked Julia.

"No, I don't have to tell him everything," said Savana. They both left the cafe and went to Julia's mother's boutique. She was surprised to see Savana. She greeted her and asked her about her parents and their trip to Sicily and Tunisia. "I was very happy to see my parents and the trips to Sicily and Tunisia were exciting and enjoyable. My parents were happy to see me and, of course, they missed me and I missed them too," Savana shared with Julia's mother.

"I will come and visit you to further discuss these rather secretive family relations," said Julia's to Savana.

"Savana, how well do you actually know Gabriele's family?" asked Julia's mother. "Julia told me while you were at Karolina's house a ,man called and Karolina went and took the call downstairs. His voice sounded like Bruno's voice. I told Julia that it was very strange that he called Karolina. She overheard him telling her about our trip to Sicily and Tunisia."

"Oh, I wish Karolina could stay away from our business!" lamented Savana.

"That's why I am here," Julia's mother replied. Julia told me to come and talk to you about Gabriele's family because something you saw in Tunisia made you really suspicious. You told Julia about it and she told me to come and see you because I know the story."

"Let me start this way. I am glad that you came to me and wanted to talk. When Julia first told me about you, I already knew who you were. I already knew that you were going to marry Gabriele. My cousin had planned all of these happenings. She planned for you to meet Gabriele. Did you celebrate your birthday at his restaurant?"

"Yes," replied Savana.

"That was her idea. She wanted to get rid of you and make you not to want to marry Jasen. Gabriele's parents and Karolina's parents were very good friends and they have so many secrets. My mother and her mother were really sisters. My advice to you, dear Savana, is to just enjoy the ride and pretend you don't know anything," suggested Julia's mother.

"Every time I spoke to Gabriele, he seemed to know all about the family and whatever was going on. Now, it all makes sense to me. Did Gabriele have a relationship before or was he married before?" asked Savana.

"OK, I am going to tell you the secrets," Julia's mother confided.

"Gabriele was married before to a Tunisian woman and he had an affair with an Italian woman. It was an ugly marriage. The woman took everything from him, money and a bunch of properties. Gabriele is a very wealthy man. He broke off his relationship with the Italian woman. Just before you came into the picture, he had been seen with another girl from Tunisia, but now I heard that they broke up too. He had been single for a while until you came into the picture," said Julia's mother.

"I noticed that every time I came here, he wanted to come too," Savana said.

"He was afraid I might tell you things about him. I am sorry Savana, that you must know these details about him. Let everything take its course and just go on with your life," said Julia's mother.

"I really appreciate you for sharing all this information with me. I had a long suspicion about Karolina and I know she has many secrets and it is driving her crazy that she cannot share it with anybody. I still think she did something to Sofi. It is really strange that all of sudden Sofi is having problem with her pregnancy. Karolina reminds me of an evil witch," said Savana.

"Well, Savana, I am glad that you finally know the truth but keep your nice personality. Everything is going to be unfolded in front of you. You just wait and watch," said Julia's mother.

"I better go home now before he starts looking for me," said Savana.

Jerry called as soon as she got home. "Hi mom!"

"I am very happy you called. How are you, my son?" asked Savana.

"I am doing very well," said Jerry. "I am going to be done in three weeks. I am not coming home right away. I have to check when my law class starts and I need to check when my next class starts next year," said Jerry.

"Have you told your father that you are going to take law?" asked Savana.

"No, I want to surprise him. How is he doing? Now that he's a married man. How's the baby?" asked Jerry.

"He is not very happy right now. I hate to tell you this. I don't think they are going to have their baby. There is something wrong with the baby ,and the doctor said that they have to remove her womb where they found cancer. They are going to try to remove the cancer, but if they can't do it, they are going to have a premature baby. Karolina has been very quiet lately. I have more stories to tell you, but let's just wait until you come home," said Savana.

"Are you ready to get married, mom?" asked Jerry.

"I don't know son, I just don't know," said Savana.

"What's wrong? You sound like you don't want to get married," said Jerry.

"Let's stop talking about this until you get home and we'll talk about it then," said Savana.

"Okay, Mom. I will see you in three weeks," said Jerry happily.

Chapter
Forty-Four

Right after Savana hung up the phone, Gabriele entered the door. They were glad to see each other and Savana asked him how his day was and he said they were very busy.

"Have you heard from Jerry? ' Gabriele asked.' He should be done with school very soon," said Savana.

"I was just talking to him before you arrived. He's done with school in three weeks and he's looking forward to coming home," said Savana.

"What did you do after school today?" asked Gabriele.

"I went with Julia to the library and did some reading. Julia then told me about Sofia's baby. She is having problems with the baby. She has cancer around the womb. The doctor is going to operate on her. He is going to operate around the uterus to remove the cancer otherwise she will need to deliver a premature baby," said Savana.

"Let's hope she and the baby are going to be all right," said Gabriele.

Savana felt that Gabriele was suspicious of her. He didn't believe her that she just had a talk with Julia. He believed that she went to see Julia's mother. He noticed that Savana's mood had changed and he suspected that she knew something. He asked Savana to come to the restaurant after school the next day to have dinner with him. She accepted and was looking forward to their dinner date. They slept through the night without discussing anything. Gabriele usually got up earlier than Savana but this time she got up first. She wanted to go to see Julia to tell her mother not to tell Gabriele that she was there the day before. She got dressed and fixed her breakfast and while she was just about to eat, Gabriele walked in and surprised her with a kiss on the cheek.

"Good morning my love!"

"That was a good surprise!" she told Gabriele.

"Thank you." "Why are you so up early today?" he asked.

"Oh, I need to spend some time preparing for our wedding," she said.

"I am glad you are going to do that. Maybe you should ask Julia and her mother to help you," he said.

"I think that is a very good idea," Savana told Gabriele. "I better run now and I will catch you later tonight at the restaurant," Savana told Gabriele. He knew she was hiding something from him. It was really strange that she left the house early that morning. He knew she went with Julia to her mother's boutique store and he knew that Julia's mother knew all the secrets of her family and himself. He just brushed it off because it was not important to him at the moment and he left for work. Savana met Julia in the village and told her that she must talk to her.

"What's wrong Savana?" she asked.

"Please, can we call your mother right now?" she said.

"Why, is there something wrong?" Julia asked.

"Gabriele was very suspicious of me last night. He asked me all kinds of questions. I noticed that for some reason, every time I am with you, he gets worried," she told Julia.

"He knows my mother knows all his family secrets including his," said Julia. "If I were you just don't worry about it. Someday, you are going to know all their secrets," said Julia. "If he asked you, just tell him that you just forgot to call him," said Julia.

"I am supposed to have dinner with him tonight. I am going straight to the restaurant from here. We want to talk about our wedding and how many guests we are inviting," said Savana.

"That is a lot of work," said Julia.

"They want to know how many guests I am inviting from America," said Savana.

They said goodbye and Savana went to the restaurant to meet Gabriele. He was happy to see his beautiful wife to be. He gave her a kiss on the cheek and told her that he missed her and she said the same.

"You had a long day and you must be very tired now," he told Savana.

"Yes, pretty much and I just want to go to bed. I am exhausted."

"Well, right now we have to talk about how many guests we are going to be inviting from your side," he told Savana. She already knew how many people she was inviting from her side. She told him about ten people.

"I have about two hundred people to invite. I have many good friends and relatives," he told her.

"That's great and I am very happy to meet them as well," she told Gabriele. "The restaurant is going to prepare the food and the dining area. It is going to be cold but the Mediterranean weather is going to be very lovely."

Savana was very happy that they took care of all the wedding matters and they could concentrate on getting ready for the wedding. Her parents would arrive one week early to celebrate Christmas together before the wedding. She was looking forward to that. Lately, Savana had been feeling very suspicious of Gabriele. She saw the change in his moods and ways towards her. Sometimes he was more passionate and showed more love towards her. She forgot her suspicious mind when he was intimate and passionate.

"Are you ready to go home?" Gabriele saw that Savana's thoughts had drifted so far away and he asked her again, "Are you ready to go home, Savana?"

"Oh! yes, yes" she replied. They went home without talking. They both went to bed tired from the day's work.

"If I have more sleep, it will give me more energy to prepare for the wedding. I want to make sure that we have all the guests that we have invited and all the food that we are to serve to the people," explained Savana to Julia the next morning at coffee.

"Let's say goodbye for now and we'll go and see my mother later on this week," Julia said to Savana.

Savana arrived home at 1:00 pm. She went and changed her clothes quickly before she went to see Gabriele at the restaurant. Her phone rang and it was Jerry.

"Hi mom! How are you?" he asked.

"How are you doing?" she asked her son.

"I am on school break now and I am all done with school," Jerry said with relief.

"When are you coming home?" she asked.

"I will be home on this Friday and I am really looking forward to coming home," he said with a little lost puppy sound.

"We are looking forward to seeing you, my son!" said Savana.

"How's your wedding preparation coming along?" he asked his mother.

"Very well," she said.

"Better say goodbye now and I will see you soon," said Jerry.

Savana rushed to the restaurant. It was packed with people. She had never seen the restaurant that busy. Gabriele saw her right away and he rushed over to her and kissed her on both cheeks. Savana was happy to see him. They missed each other and especially because

Savana spent all day in preparations for the wedding and Gabriele spent all his day at the restaurant.

"This is a nice surprise that you come and see me at work," he told Savana.

"I missed you and I always want to see you and now I will have to see you all the time. I talked to Jerry for a few minutes and he is coming home on Friday," she said excitedly.

"That's a very good news to hear," Gabriele said.

"I want to go to Julia's mother's boutique tomorrow to look at some dresses and shoes. My mom wanted a dress. She is not sure what to wear to the wedding," she said.

"What time are you planning to go there?" Gabriele asked her.

Chapter
Forty-Five

"About 10:00 am Julia is coming to pick me up," Savana informed Gabriele.

"Call me or come and see me at the restaurant," he said.

"I was planning on it," she said faithfully.

Savana saw the changes in Gabriele. He showed more love towards her. She also noticed that they made love for a very long time. She went with Julia the next day to her mother's boutique. She was very happy to see Savana.

"Are you excited to get married?" she asked Savana.

"Yes, I am very excited and I am really looking forward to it," Savana squealed in delight.

"I just found your mother a beautiful dress," said Julia's mother.

Savana took a glance at the dress. She was very happy with how beautiful the mother of the bride's dress was. She told Julia's mother that she would like to buy it. It was a light blue silk brocade dress with little white flowers on it. It was a beautiful dress. She went to meet Gabriele at the restaurant to get something to eat before they got home. Gabriele asked her if she found a dress for her mother.

"Yes, I found the perfect dress for my mom. It is a light blue dress with white flowers -and blue is her favorite color."

They talked about the wedding for a while. "They were going to have so many guests coming to their wedding.

"I have some relatives from England and Spain who are coming and we have not seen them for years," said Gabriele.

"I noticed new employees at the restaurant," observed Savana.

"I hired thirty more new people to work here and in Sicily. We are going to need more people to help in Sicily for the wedding," said Gabriele. They were both tired and went to bed. Savana did not have to get up early but Gabriele had to get up. He had some more interviews to do that day. He left early that morning to go to work. He did not wake up Savana but left her a note to call when she woke up.

She was awakened by the phone call. She picked it up and it was her darling son.

"Hi mom, did I wake you up?" he asked.

"Jerry! I am very happy to hear you voice," she told Jerry.

"I am glad to hear your voice as well," he replied. "I just want to tell you that I am coming home tomorrow."

"I am glad to hear that and I am really looking forward to seeing you my son," she said. "My wedding day is getting closer and I want to talk to you about my situation with Gabriele," she said.

"We'll talk tomorrow, mom," Jerry said to his mother.

Savana was very excited about Jerry's arrival and she walked over to Gabriele and broke the good news to him.

"My son is arriving tomorrow Gabriele and I very excited to see him," she told him.

"I am very happy to see him too," said Gabriele. He hugged Savana and kissed her on her cheek. "What time is he arriving?" asked Gabriele.

"He is flying right now and he is arriving at six o'clock tomorrow morning," she said.

"Wow! That's early! We might as well stay up and not sleep," he said.

They both went to bed and felt excited about Jerry's arrival. Gabriele set the alarm clock for 4:30am. They both said good night to one another. Savana stayed awake all night as well as Gabriele. The alarm went off and they were up right way. They both cleaned themselves, got dressed, and drank some coffee and off they drove to the airport to meet Jerry. They arrived at the airport at 5 a. m They had to have more coffee while waiting. Savana was very sleepy and closed her eyes and waited. Finally, they announced Jerry's flight had just landed. Savana, got up from her sleep and she started looking at the passengers coming out one by one. She finally saw her son Jerry coming. She could not wait so she ran over and hugged him with tears and kissed him.

"Welcome home, son," she told Jerry.

He was very excited and happy to see his mom. Gabriele walked over and hugged him. They noticed that Jerry had grown taller than the last time they saw him. Jerry was glad to see both of them. He got in the car with them and they drove off home.

Gabriele told them he wanted to take them for breakfast. They got home and Jerry settled in. He took his shower, got dressed and he was ready to go for breakfast. Gabriele took them to a wonderful restaurant. They served all kinds of Italian foods. Jerry asked them if they were excited that their wedding was drawing closer.

"I am excited and looking forward to marry your mom," said Gabriele.

"How about you, mom?" he asked his mother.

"I am very excited and I can't wait to marry your new dad," said Savana. "This weekend we are going to Sicily to check everything out and make sure all looks perfect for the wedding."

After breakfast, Gabriele went to work while Savana and Jerry went home to do some catching up with school and the wedding plans.

"You both look very happy," said Jerry.

"We are both very happy and we can't wait to get married and you and I have a lot to talk about," said Savana.

"Let's go and have something to eat and we'll talk. I can't wait to hear what you are going to tell me mother."

They found a nice coffee place near the ocean, and even though the breeze was cold the sun felt warm. Jerry ordered some pastries, toast, eggs and some coffee and orange juice. They both sat down and had their breakfast. They both talked about schools and what they were going to do in the coming year.

"I am not going to take up law, but I just want to finish my degree and come home and work," he told his mother.

How come you changed your mind son?" asked Savana.

"I have to continue my school for another four years and I don't want to do that mom. I will be going to school for ever. I want to work and make money and take care of you," he said to his mother.

"Thank you for always thinking about me, son," said Savana. "I am always proud of you, Jerry. I can't wait to see you making money," said his mother. "I want to tell you a secret about Gabriele. He is a very nice man, but he has some deep secrets. He was married before and he is divorced now. We just recently went to Tunisia, a Muslim country. This was during the time your grandfather and grandmother came to visit. Gabriele thought it would be really nice to take them there. While we were walking on the beach, Gabriele was gone. To my surprise I saw him talking with a woman. I walked quickly to him and asked him why did he just leave us in a very strange land. He said good bye to the girl and we walked over to my parents. All of a sudden, I saw a strange look on his face. I told him that we should go home because it was getting late. Gabriele was very quiet on the way home. We left your grandparents at their hotel and we left for home. I did not say anything on the way home at all. We both felt very tired and when we got home, we said good night and went to sleep. On the next day, my parents had to fly back to America. We said good bye and off they went back home. We had to fly back here. I had to go back to planning the wedding and he had to go to work."

Chapter Forty-Six

The next day I went shopping. Julia came to eat lunch with me and I told her that I wanted to see her mother. We planned we should go and see her. I told her mother the story about the girl he met at Tunisia. She then told me this strange story about Gabriele. He was married to a girl from there but it got ugly so he decided to divorce her. I heard that he had a new girlfriend from there too.

"That could make sense too about this girl that she saw with him," Savana said. "She looked like my age," she said. "She has long black hair and she was tall," she told Jerry. "I could not take a picture of her because she was so far away."

"Is she going to be at the wedding?" asked Jerry.

"I really don't know but I have to see the list of the guests," said Savana. "Let's go and see Julia's mom boutique store. I want to introduce you to her and Julia," said Savana. Julia's mom was very happy to meet Jerry.

Oh, you are a very good-looking young man and you look just like your dad," she told him. "Are you having a school break now?" Julia's mother asked.

"Yes, I am having a school break and I am very excited that my mom and Gabriele are going to get married," he told her. "Has my mom invited you yet?" he asked.

"Oh! Yes, we are definitely coming." "Have you seen your grandmother Karolina yet?" Julia's mother inquired. I am sure that she would love to see you, Jerry," she added.

"I am planning to go and see them both tomorrow," Jerry responded.

We are going to Sicily this weekend," he said.

"She was thinking about you yesterday; Karolina knows you are here now. She asked your dad if you are already here," she said.

"I brought them both presents," he said.

Savana's phone was ringing and it was Gabriele. He wanted to know where they were. He asked them to come over to the restaurant and have dinner with him. They had to leave right away and they headed to see him. He was happy to see them. They sat down and had pasta, salmon and salad. Jerry told Gabriele that he was going to see his dad and grandmother the next day.

"That's very nice that you are going to see them. They both have missed you." Gabriele said.

Savana noticed some new workers in the restaurant. There was one in particular who looked very interesting to her. She did not want to bother Gabriele. She kept looking at her and the girl stared back at her. She moved quickly to serve the next table.

She knew that was the same girl on the beach with Gabriele. This must be the old girlfriend. This is strange that she was working at the restaurant. Karolina must have planned this. She told Gabriele that she was going home with Jerry and she was feeling tired. They went home and she did not say a word to Jerry. When they got home, she told Jerry that she wanted to tell him something. She asked her son to sit down.

"I want to tell you that the girl I was telling you about- I saw her tonight."

"How mom? Is she a Muslim and from Tunisia? And how did she get here?" asked Jerry.

"I want you to listen very carefully to me," Savana said.

"Gabriele used to have a girlfriend before me. She used to work in the same restaurant and Gabriele was going to marry her and guess who stopped the wedding?" asked Savana.

Jerry knew the answer right away. "Grandma Karolina," he replied.

"Very good, my son," said Savana.

"Are you going to ask Gabriele?" asked Jerry.

"No, I'm not going to. I am going to stay out when Karolina is involved with something, it's going to be ugly. Karolina just doesn't like me."

She wants to get rid of me. She doesn't want me to be happy," said Savana. "You see, they know each other very well. They knew Karolina's father and Karolina was supposed to marry his dad and she married someone else who happened to be your dad's father."

Karolina has a big secret. Her grandfather joined a gang and he was involved with dirty money worth millions and millions of dollars. It made your grandfather one of the wealthiest men in Sicily. Gabriele's grandfather too was very wealthy and he was involved with dirty money. His brother is one of the most powerful attorneys in Sicily. He started cracking down with gang members and their dirty business," explained Savana.

"This is the main reason why I want to be a lawyer," said Jerry. "I want to prosecute all these gang members and criminals. I already signed up to take law next year.

They heard the door open and it was Gabriele. 'You guys are still up?"

"We are still doing some catching up," said Jerry.

"I am excited to go back to Sicily and check out all the wedding celebration plans and to make sure everything is in the right place," said Gabriele.

"How many guests are you expecting?" asked Jerry.

"About 500 guests," he said.

"There will be a lot of people.," said Jerry.

"I have relatives all over the world and they are happy to hear that I am marrying an American woman and they are all excited," he said.

The phone was ringing, and Savana grabbed the phone really fast and answered it. She said "Hello" and she recognized that very familiar voice.

It was Karolina. "Hi Savana! I have not seen you for a very long time, maybe we should have lunch or something. I heard that my grandson is here. I want to talk to him."

"Let me get him to talk to you." Savana gave Jerry the phone.

"Hi Grandma! How are you doing?"

"I am very happy to hear your voice, Jerry. I was asking your dad when are you going to be home and he told me that you are here now.

" I am coming to see you and dad tomorrow. I have presents from Harvard for both of you," Jerry told Karolina.

"I am looking forward to seeing you, Jerry" she said to him. They said good bye.

"She misses you very much, Jerry," said Gabriele.

How well do you know Karolina?" asked Jerry.

"I have known her family since I was born. Her father used to be my grandfather's best friend. They used to visit each other and travel together. She was supposed to marry my father but she went and married someone else. The main problem was that she did not want to live in Sicily," he said. "She's like my real mother. I did not really know Jasen because when I was just born, he was already in college. Your father went to Harvard medical school."

Jerry responded to Gabriele with a sense of independence: "My dad suggested for me to go to the same school. I told him that I don't want to be a doctor like him. So, I chose Harvard business school instead."

"We should go to bed now; tomorrow is another busy day," Gabriele suggested kindly.

Jerry was getting close to asking Gabriele about his past life, but he decided to wait until they were in Sicily. Jerry was very protective of his mom and Gabriele already knew that. They all said goodnight to one another and went to sleep. Jerry stayed up thinking about everything his mother had told him, and he was not sleepy because of the time differences between America and Italy. Savana could not go to sleep either due to her anxiety.

She was thinking of what she saw at the restaurant and Gabriele had not told her anything about it. She decided to it let it go for now. Gabriele had the same problem. He could not go to sleep. He was really thinking about their wedding. He worried about Savana, about his secrets: What if she knows his secrets and most importantly was the knowledge about Jerry. He was worried how many more questions he was going to ask him. He pretended that he was going to sleep but really, he was wide awake. They all had secrets about those who dwelled in this house and the secrets were about to be revealed.

Jerry was up at nine am. He pulled his curtains open and the sunshine hit his face and felt good. He went to take a quick shower, got dressed and went to the kitchen where Gabriele and Savana were.

He leaned over to his mother and kissed her forehead and he said to Gabriele as well: "I am going over to see my dad at his office and Karolina wants to take us for breakfast," he told Savana and Gabriele.

Gabriele left for work and said good bye to both of them. Now, they were alone again, and had a chance to talk freely in the house.

"Mom, have you ever thought that Gabriele might be taping our conversation when we are alone in the house?" Jerry asked.

"You know what son, last night I thought about that. I could not go to sleep at all last night. After seeing that girl in the restaurant, I felt that something was going to happen at the wedding. I don't know why I am thinking this way. I also felt that he is recording our conversations and I feel terrible about it but guess what? He has secrets too that he does not want to share," Savana said.

They both paused for a while and Jerry heard his echo which is the sign that someone is recording you. He asked his mom to keep talking because he was going to look where the tape was located.

Jerry started looking around the kitchen. He looked at the kitchen counter in the corner and saw a little microphone was hidden there. He called his mother to come over to see what he had found.

He warned her: "I don't want you to confront him yet. He might really turn out to be against us. Karolina must have had him tape us. Karolina is evil and dirty. I think that is what his grandfather taught her to do."

"She wants me to disappear. Gabriele is on her side. How evil these people are. Now, we know that we are recorded, to let them know what we are talking about. Now he will hear about that girl that I am very curious about. I am coming with you. I have not seen your dad for a very long time as well as Karolina," said Savana to Jerry. They left to see Jasen and Karolina.

"This is a nice surprise to see both of you here. It has been a long time not to see the both of you," said Jasen. "Son, you've grown into a tall and very nice-looking boy. Do you have a girlfriend yet?" his father asked. Jerry laughed so loud.

"I am not looking for a girlfriend! I have been studying really hard, dad."

Savana, your wedding is coming up very soon. Have you and Gabriele finished all the wedding plans?" Jasen inquired politely.

"Yes, we are going over to Sicily tomorrow to check all the wedding details and to make sure that everything is working well."

Karolina arrived and surprised them. She was very happy to see Jerry her grandson and Savana. She kissed both of them.

"Savana your wedding is coming up very soon," said Karolina.

"Yes, we are leaving for Sicily tomorrow. We want to check everything and we will be there for another week before my parents arrive from America," said Savana.

"That must be really nice," said Karolina. "Are you ready for breakfast?" asked Karolina. "You might as well come with us."

Chapter
Forty-Seven

Savana noticed both Jasen and Karolina missed her and Jerry. It was really nice to see both of them and share some stories with them.

"How is school Jerry?" Karolina asked.

"School is great grandma. This is my final semester and I will be graduating in June of next year!"

"You are going to be a grown man. I remember you when you were a small baby, but now you are going to be done with college and get a job somewhere. You probably have a girlfriend now," said Karolina.

Jerry burst out laughing again when he heard her say that.

"No grandmother, I don't have a girlfriend yet. I am thinking of going back to school and studying law," he said.

"You what! Did you hear that, Jasen?" asked Karolina

"Yes, I heard and if I can do it, he can do it!". It is up to Jerry now. He is very smart and I am sure he is going to be a very good lawyer," said Jasen.

"I hope you are not going to school for the rest of your life," said Karolina sarcastically.

"Oh! no, no grandma. I will be done in fifteen months."

"Well, I have a doctor's appointment now, but I hope to see you again sooner than before, Jerry!" said Karolina as she prepared to leave,

As Karolina closed the door, Savana asked : "Jasen how is your small family?"

"My wife is going to lose the baby and that's sad," Jasen said.

"What is wrong with the baby?" Savana asked.

"The doctor said he has some kind of disease that is going to jeopardize the mother's health. The scary part is as the baby grows the disease keeps growing at the same time," said Jasen.

"This is horrible!" "Has she talked to her parents and family. Maybe they had some strange disease and no one wanted to talk about it." "What are you going to do now?" asked Savana.

"Nothing, nothing can be done," said Jasen defeated and sad.

Changing the topic that weighed heavy on his soul, Jasen commented to Savana: "Your wedding is approaching really fast. I am glad Jerry will have a chance to see his American family!"

"My parents went to visit him in Harvard and he was very happy to see them," said Savana.

"How is Karolina doing?" Savan asked politely. "I noticed that she is slowing down now. Maybe because I haven't seen her for a very long time," observed Savana.

"No, she has slowed down a lot," Jasen answered. "She was admitted into the hospital two months ago."

"What was wrong with her?" Savana asked.

"She got dizzy and fell down and broke her arm," said Jasen.

"I think your mother is getting too old. I had no idea that you grew up with Gabriele's family," said Savana.

"Oh, yes, we grew up together. We know his parents and grandparents and their great grandparents. My mother was always close to them- even now," said Jasen.

"That makes sense to me," Savana reflected.

"Did you know that Gabriele and Karolina are very close?" asked Savana.

"Yes, I always knew that. They have a secret and I have no idea what is it," said Jasen.

"I hope they are not planning a bad event to happen at the wedding!" Savana blushed as she blurted out her suspicion. "We better go now, before Gabriele starts looking for us," said Savana. They all said good bye to one another and left.

They got home late and they prepared some salad really fast but Gabriele showed up with their dinner. "Did you just get home?" Gabriele asked.

"Yes, I went with Jerry to see his father."

"How is Jasen doing?" he asked Savana.

"He was telling us about his wife and the baby which is not very good news to tell you."

"What happened?" asked Gabriele.

"In order for the mother to survive, they have to let go of the baby. The baby has some kind of blood disorder. The disease keeps on spreading," said Savana. "The doctors cannot figure out what kind of blood disorder it is," said Savana.

"Well, Jasen is a doctor; can he help them?" asked Gabriele.

"He has to have an Italian license in order for him to help them," said Savana.

"I feel sorry for both of them- this is Sofi's first baby and it is such a sad thing." Gabriele agreed.

"But on the brighter side of life, I am very excited that my parents are arriving on Friday and Jerry gets to spend some time with them," said Savana.

'Yes, time really flies," said Gabriele.

Gabriele left early to go to work while Jerry and his mother decided to go out for breakfast.

"I want to talk with your dad to day. I have some questions that I need to ask him before the wedding," said Savana to Jerry.

"What kind of questions, Mom?" Jerry asked.

"About my husband to be," replied Savana.

"I will call him right now for you," said Jerry. "Hi dad! Are you going to be busy today?" asked Jerry.

"No, not really. Why?" asked Jasen.

"Mom wants to talk to you.

"Is she with you now?' asked Jasen.

"Yes, she is right here," replied Jerry.

"You both can come here and talk to me," said Jasen.

"Where is grandma today?" asked Jerry.

"She has another doctor's appointment," said Jasen.

Jerry told him that they were coming right away.

"Well Savana what is on your mind. Yesterday you looked worried," said Jasen.

"I have been worrying about Gabriele because I had a feeling he is going to leave me after the wedding and go to that Muslim woman who is working at the restaurant now," said Savana.

"I should warn you Savana that Gabriele loves Muslim women. They are very mysterious according to him. I think his first wife was a Muslim," Jasen surmised. "He is very close to my mother and she is not very friendly when she hears your name mentioned. She is the one who did not want us to get married. Look at her choice now; she ends up in a very sad situation," said Jasen.

"My advice to you is to just go with the flow and pretend you do not know anything," said Jasen to Savana.

"I am not even scared of anything. My parents and their best friends from America are going to be here soon," said Savana. "Jasen, shall I tell them what is happening here?" asked Savana.

"No, they are going to call the wedding off," said Jasen.

"The woman is going to work in the restaurant where the wedding celebration is going to be held," said Savana. "I am not surprised.

"Are you going to invite us to come to the wedding?" asked Jasen.

"I was not going to invite you at first but now I will," said Savana. "Gabriele already invited my mom and she will be really surprised that you've invited me to come to the wedding."

"As matter of fact, I brought you two invitation cards," said Savana.

"I will let my wife know and thank you very much for the invitation and we will be there. I can't wait to see your parents again," said Jasen.

Jerry and Savana went and did a little shopping before they returned home. She bought some perfumes and bath soaps for her mother and some cologne for her father. Gabriele was waiting for them when they got home.

"We have been shopping," said Jerry.

He already brought their dinner and they all sat down and ate. They were very inward and quiet.

"How was your day, Gabriele?" Savana asked almost in a whisper.

"We were really busy today. There were many American tourists and that was nice. We had many tourists from Europe as well and your parents are arriving tomorrow with the rest of your family," said Gabriele.

"My family has a great sense of humor. They tell so many jokes. You are going to enjoy them," said Savana.

"We have to go to bed early tonight because we have a very busy day tomorrow," said Gabriele.

Savana could not go sleep as she thought about what Jasen told her during their visit during the day. She is marrying a man who does not really love her. She is scared of him now. He is going back to his previous lover. How is he going to go with her when he's marrying me? She asked that question to herself. Whatever is going to happen they will show up. Like Jasen told her to just go with the flow. The face of that woman she will never forget -the way she looked at her in the restaurant the last time- she could never forget. It is like a photographic memory has been planted in her brain. She kept tossing around on the bed and she stood up like the woman was sleeping with them and she screamed and woke both Gabriele and Jerry. She walked out from the bedroom to the living room.

"What is wrong mom? I heard you scream," observed Jerry in a shocked tone.

Gabriele came over and hugged her. "What happened did you have a nightmare?" asked Gabriele.

"I could not go to sleep and I kept seeing this woman's face. I was scared of her and I screamed." said Savana.

"What woman did you see?" asked Gabriele.

"The woman from Tunisia. She has long black hair," explained Savana.

"She is one of the new employees that I recently hired. There were forty of them. She is going to be working at the restaurant in Sicily during the wedding dinner," said Gabriele.

"It is about time for us to be honest with one another. I don't really know anything about you except that you own these restaurants all over the world. I know you are Karolina's best friend and I can imagine that she arranges all these secret encounters for you to fall in love with me and marry me to avoid Jasen," accused Savana suspiciously.

"How could you say that? That is not fair that you are blaming me for all these situations," said Gabriele.

"I am very suspicious of Karolina's motives and I know she has something to do with this!" whimpered Savana.

Chapter Forty-Eight

"That Muslim girl was your ex-lover and didn't you marry one from Tunisia as well? I heard that you like those Muslim girls; they're very mysterious," Savana cried out deeply wounded in her heart by his betrayal l to confide his truth to her.

She was American and did not understand the old world patriarchy and their treatment of women.

Gabriele was very upset at Savana's accusatory mocking voice. He got dressed and went silently fuming to the restaurant.

"Well, Jerry, I confronted him and he won't tell me the truth," Savana told Jerry with a suppressed sob that echoed and thumped with a hollow sound in her hurting chest.

"This is not the right time to bring up something like that. Grandpa and Grandma are arriving this morning and what are you going to tell them?" asked Jerry.

"Let's get dressed and go to the airport to meet them and go with them to their hotel," said Savana. "If they ask for him, I will just tell them that he is working."

They arrived at the airport about 10:00 a.m..The plane touched down and the passengers started to deplane. They were standing there anxiously and finally Jerry saw his grandfather, his uncle Mike and his wife, his aunt Rose, and his uncle Mark who is an attorney now. Savana has three brothers who are all lawyers and her younger sister who is also an attorney. They all very happy to see Savana and Jerry. Her parents asked about Gabriele and she told them that he was busy working at his restaurant.

"When are we going to see this handsome Italian man?" his brother Mark asked laughing at the same time.

"Very soon," replied Savana.

They all went to their hotel to unpack their suitcases. Savana's phone was ringing and it was Gabriele. He asked her if they had arrived. Savana told him they had arrived on time.

"I want you to bring them to have breakfast or lunch. I will wait for all of you here," Gabriele graciously replied. Savana thanked him.

"Gabriele just called and he wants us all to come to the restaurant and have a delicious Italian brunch," said Savana."

Gabriele greeted them and they were very happy to meet him and they all sat down before brunch was served.

"I am impressed Savana. He is very handsome and what a beautiful restaurant," said her brother Mark. Gabriele came and sat next to Savana.

"This is a beautiful restaurant, Gabriele," said Savana's dad.

"I come from Sicily where we are going to have the wedding," Gabriele replied. My parents and the rest of my family love Karolina there. I have two brothers who are also lawyers. One of them is really powerful. He tried to stop all different kinds of gangs in Sicily. It is a lot better to live in Sicily now. It is much safer and more beautiful."

"We will all be going over to Sicily at the end of the week. That way you'll have a chance to meet my family and have a tour of my father's vineyard and do some wine tasting. We live close by your hotel and you can come by and look at our house and we can go down to the beach even though it is cold, but the Mediterranean weather and the sea breeze are very good for you," said Gabriele.

"We'll do that" replied Savana's mother. They thanked Gabriele for the nice breakfast and lunch. Gabriele invited them again for dinner with their friends. Gabriele told Savana that he wanted to talk to her and he would talk to her later and visit with her family.

"I will see you later at the hotel," said Savana.

"That was very nice of him to invite us to his restaurant," said Savana's mother.

"Did you notice something about Savana?" Mark asked. "She did not look very happy today. "Do you know anything about why Jerry?"

"I overhead mom was confronting Gabriele about something and he just got dressed and went to work this morning. That was the first time I heard mom confront him," Jerry said, trying to cover for his mom's unfortunate and awkward situation with her soon to be husband. They all went to the hotel and unpacked their suitcases and took a shower and took some naps.

"Our house is just walking distance from here. As a matter of fact, you can see it from here," said Jerry.

They all went outside and looked as Jerry pointed to the house. "He has a beautiful house," his Aunty Rose said. They all went back to their room and sat down and talked about Savana and Gabriele.

"He seemed to be a very nice guy for Savana," Savana's mother said. "We know they both look madly in love with each other, but Gabriele wanted to clear the air and he asked Savana to stay behind so they could talk," she added.

"Do you think he has someone else?" asked Mark.

"Jerry probably knows everything that is going on," said Mike.

"Uncle Mark. I don't know their life style because I have been away at school. When I would call Mom once in a while, I could tell that sometimes she sounded sad. The problem is she didn't explain or talk about their problems to me. For example, last night she just got on Gabriele, but she didn't explain herself very well. Early this morning, Gabriele got dressed and left in a huff. We were supposed to come and meet all of you but she got mad at Gabriele," explained Jerry.

"When are the rest of the wedding party going to get here?" asked Jerry.

"Your grandpa went to meet them at the airport," said Rose.

"We are all going to have dinner at the restaurant tonight. "Is Savana coming here?" asked Mark.

"They are going to show up here very soon," said Jerry.

"Have you heard that he ever cheated on mother?" asked Mark.

"Well, Uncle Mark, I just heard rumors that he was married to a Muslim girl and he left her but I am going to let my mother tell you the rest of the story," said Jerry.

"What story?" asked Rose.

"They are very good friends with Karolina and she has many secrets," said Jerry. "Well, well grandpa has arrived with his friends!"

"Is this little Jerry? Wow, you are a handsome boy! How is Harvard?"

"I am enjoying it and I am going to be graduating very soon. I am going to enter law school after that," said Jerry.

"I am glad to hear that, Jerry," said Jerry's Grandpa.

"Here they come, Gabriele and Savana," alerted Jerry.

They all greeted them and Savana's dad introduced his friends to Gabriele and Savana. "I am very glad to meet all of you," said Gabriele.

Savana just said "Hello" to all of them as well. They talked about Italy and the United States and how the culture was very different and interestingly enough, how most Americans have an Italian heritage. Most Italian- Americans are very adaptable to the Italian culture, they explained to Gabriele. Savana's whole family background was mostly Italian.

Gabriele was very surprised to hear this information and said, "The first time I saw Savana, I fell in love with her right away. She is the most beautiful woman I have ever seen," said Gabriele. "I saw a very strong Italian look in her but when I heard that she was American, I was glad to know this too." Turning to make eye contact with Jerry, Gabriele asked: "Has Jerry shown our house to you all? We live very close to this hotel and it is just walking distance from here," said Gabriele.

"Yes, Jerry showed it to us and what a beautiful house it is," said Rose.

"My house in Sicily is more exquisite than this. It is near the sound and the salty air of the Mediterranean Sea. I also have a 300 foot sail boat where we are going to have our honeymoon," said Gabriele. "I will give a tour of the boat before the wedding," Gabriele added with machismo pride.

The restaurant just called me that the dinner is ready," Gabriele told them. "I am going to leave now, but I want to check first to make sure everything is right."

He rushed off to the restaurant.

"What a good-looking man and so nice, Savana. You are very lucky to have met him."

He is very polite but he is a typical bravado Sicilian machismo man," said Mike smiling and winking at his sister.

Savana thanked her brother for his "nice" comment about Gabriele. They were all dressed up and left for the restaurant. Gabriele had already reserved a special room for them. The restaurant was perfect. It had a very nice view of the ocean. They admired everything about the place. Starting from the furniture, the beautiful flowers, the paintings on the wall, the smell of fresh bread baking, and the beautiful people who worked there. They were served first with Italian wine, pasta, salad, and they were given a choice of steak or fish as their second course.

"You are very lucky Savana that you met this man, and I am very proud of you for always showing your respectful nature and kindness," commented her father.

After dinner, they were served a popular dessert *cassata*, a Sicilian cake made with Ricotta cheese and an Italian liqueur made with almonds, called *Amaretto*. They left the restaurant at 11:00 pm to go back to their hotel before they all departed for Sicily for the wedding. Savana stayed behind at the restaurant with her future husband. Jerry already left to go home. Gabriele sat next to Savana and just stared at the ocean and the moon shining, which looked like silver drops on the ocean. They sat there quietly and stared at each other's beautiful deep blue eyes. Each of them could read into each other's eyes and they could tell what kind of future was waiting for them. After all that staring and reflecting, they decided to go home for the night.

"We have another busy day tomorrow; we must finally go home to get ready for our wedding," said Gabrielle tenderly to Savana.

"Yes, I am very excited that we are going to get married finally!" said Savana.

They hugged and kissed each other. Savana was crying tears of happiness when she expressed with some confusion: "Gabriele, I love you very much! "Why am I feeling that I am going to lose you?" she passionately asked her handsome lover.

"Oh! Savana why are you asking me this question? I am not going to lose you," answered Gabriele abruptly. "Let's go home and sleep for tomorrow is going to be another long day."

Jerry was already waiting for them. "Mom, what time are we leaving tomorrow?" he asked.

"We are leaving at noon tomorrow," replied Savana.

They all went to bed for the night. Savana again, could not go to sleep. She was thinking about the wedding, the woman, Karolina and Gabriele. She knew her intuition was always right. The woman appeared in her dream again. She was telling her to enjoy Gabriele now, because he was going to leave her and she got up and left the bedroom and she walked over to the living room. She saw Jerry was sitting in the darkness.

"Mom! What are you doing here?" asked Jerry.

"I had a strange dream about that mysterious woman," said Savana. "What are you doing here Jerry?" asked his mother.

"I was having nightmares about Gabriele. I saw him jump into the ocean and disappear. I just don't know what happened to him. I also saw Grandma Karolina and another woman. Her face was very vivid for me to see. All of sudden, I saw Gabriele with them. A very strange dream," said Jerry.

"You saw a lot of things, Jerry," confirmed Savana. "My premonition unfortunately is always right," said Savana.

"I too have a feeling mom that something horrible is going to happen at the wedding," said Jerry.

"Before we left the restaurant tonight, Gabriele and I were there looking in each other's eyes and all of sudden tears just rolled down my cheeks. I asked him why am I having tears coming down on my cheeks? Why am I having this ill feeling that you are going to disappear? He just brushed it off," she told Jerry.

"We still have time to really watch his every move, everyone he speaks with and how he is handling the guests," Jerry told his mom.

"You are right Jerry. As a matter of fact, that woman is going to be working at the party that night. We must pay attention to his and her moves," advised Savana.

"This is horrible mom. There's no reason for her to be doing this to you," said Jerry.

"Guess who is planning all these evil deeds? Karolina! That is how much this woman hates me. She doesn't want me to be happy but she wants me to stay miserable like her," lamented Savana. "We are leaving tomorrow my son. You and I should stay alert. We should not trust anyone and stay alert," Savana told Jerry.

The trip back to Sicily was a lot of fun. Most of Savana's father's friends had never been to Sicily. They were looking forward to it.

When they arrived at the airport, Gabriele's father was there to greet them and welcome them to Sicily. They all admired how beautiful the town was. The hotel they were going to stay in was near a quaint ocean cove. They all checked in to their hotel and unpacked their suitcases. They decided to take a walk down to the beach to check out all the different stores and restaurants. Gabriele took Savana and Jerry to their house and hurried back to his restaurant. Jerry unpacked his clothes and helped his mother unpack all her wedding clothes. They both followed their family and friends down to the beach. Savana could see the 300-foot yacht anchored in the ocean nearby. She told her family about it.

"Gabriele said that he was going to show us around the yacht when we got here," said Mark excitedly.

"Gabriele said that he will come and join us soon, but first he wants to check to make sure the food is ready.

"Have you been inside the boat Savana?" asked her other brother Mike.

"Jerry and I have been inside. It is very beautiful. You think you are living in a floating house," said Savana.

'Here comes Gabriele," announced Savana.

"Is everyone ready to tour the boat?" asked Gabriele. They all rode in this little boat to take them to the yacht. Finally, everyone was inside the yacht. "This is the boat where Savana and I are going to have our honeymoon. We are going to sail the ocean for a couple of days and then back home," said Gabriele.

They were all surprised. Her mother looked at Savana and observed that she didn't look very happy."

What is wrong Savana?" asked her brother Mark later when they were alone with just their family at the hotel.

"I have nothing to say" said Savana to her brother.

"I have to tell you this. You have not been looking happy since we got here, can you tell us why," said Mark. "If you have something to tell us or know about Gabriele or something else, Savana you better tell us!" Her brother warned: "You looked very happy the last time we saw you but now, you look very unhappy and worried and unsettled. We are really worried about you. There must be something that happened that you are hiding from us.

"Like you have a forbidden fruit or secrets that you just cannot share with us," said her sister Rose.

"We are lawyers Savana and you just can't hide anything from us," said her brother Mike.

"One day I will tell you the secrets but not now. I will tell you this that something horrible is going to happened. I am not going to have a husband and I have a very strong feeling about it. I had dreams about misfortune and I cried about it," said Savana."

I know that Karolina does not like you. She wants you to be miserable the rest of your life and why is that Savana?" asked her brother.

"Because she controls all of them," said Savana.

"What are you talking about? Who does she control?" asked Mike.

Gabriele walked in. They ended the conversation right away.

"Are you all ready to go and have your dinner at the restaurant?" asked Gabriele.

They all said yes. They just walked from the beach to the restaurant. Jerry reminded his mother to start looking around when they got to the restaurant. The restaurant was full. Gabriele had prepared a special place for them. They all sat down while the waitress brought their food. Savana looked around and she saw the girl. Their eyes met and she quickly turned back. Savana could not take her eyes off from her. Gabriele saw Savana was staring at the girl. He went to the kitchen looking at Savana from there. His mind was thinking quickly: What If Savana's suspicion was right all along but he just ignored it? How is he going to explain to her when they got home. He knew that he had a secret that he could not share with Savana. If she knew about it, she would not marry him.

Chapter
Forty-Nine

Their dinner was over, so they decided to go back to their hotel. "I am coming with you all," said Savana.

They noticed that many new guests stayed at their hotel too. Most of them were coming to the wedding. Gabriele had family attending from all over Europe. Savana was very happy to see all her family and very close friends. She had some secrets that she could not tell anyone. Jerry knew most of them from his father, Jasen. Savana told Jerry that Jasen was going to be at the wedding as well. His mother Karolina did not even know. She would be surprised to see him.

The following night Gabriele invited the two parents to have dinner alone with them. They all went to the restaurant and had dinner there. It was a typical Italian dinner with pasta, salad and seafood with Gabriele's famous pistachio gelato for dessert.

"You have treated us very well including my family and friends. I must thank you from the bottom of our hearts," said Savana's father.

Gabriele responded back: "I am very happy to marry your beautiful daughter. I felt so lucky when I first met her! I felt that

I just met the most beautiful girl in the world. She is so kind and loving and I hope we are going to have a wonderful life together!" Savana cried after he spoke. She knew he was lying.

He would be gone after the honeymoon. She had no idea where Gabriele was going only that he and Karolina knew. She wanted to tell the secret that he was hiding, but she did not want to spoil the wedding and so she would just let her family witness whatever would tragically happen on their own.

"Why are you crying Savana?" asked Gabriele. Savana had nothing to say. They finished their dinner and Savana suggested that they should go to bed early and get ready for the wedding. Savana went with her parents. She missed her parents and her two brothers and her sister. She had been away from them for a long time. She wanted to catch up with the news from home.

Jerry was already there talking to his uncles. They all sat around the fire place at the hotel and talked.

"Are you really ready to wed this old-world man, Savana?" asked Mike.

"To be really honest with you, I don't know how to answer your question," replied Savana.

"I saw your sad face when we arrived; you did not look happy at all. I told mom right away. She said the same thing."

Her brother Mark asked: "Is this having to do with Karolina, Savana? I know she hates you and wants to get rid of you."

What I gathered was that she must have something to do with this wedding," said Mike. "How old is Karolina?" Mike asked.

"She is 80 years old and she has a lot of power," said Savana. "She got rid of me so I would not marry Jasen. Jasen married Sophia which was his choice. Now Sophia is having complications with her pregnancy. The doctor told her if she wants to live, she has to get rid of the baby. She is an evil and selfish old lady," said Savana. "She knew Gabriele's father and the grandfather and the great grandfather. She was supposed to marry his father but she went and married someone else -so they said. But she mysteriously sailed to America to give birth to Jasen. It is said that her name is the only one listed on his birth certificate although she asserts that she married someone by the name of Ricardo who claimed to be related to the Italian throne. Her parents were involved with dirty money. They were involved with gang members like Gabriele's great grandfather. They owned all of Sicily. His brother was a lawyer and he worked with law enforcement to get rid of the mob or at least stop them from using dirty money," explained Savana.

"Are they still operating?" asked her brother.

"Some are still defrauding in criminal activity, but it has not been as bad in the last ten years," said Savana. "Karolina is involved in all of these criminal activities. She has a secret about all of them and they are afraid of her because she could expose them and tell all the world," Savana confided.

"Well, my sister, do you really want to hear what I am going to tell you?" asked Mike.

"No, not really- but tell me anyway- let me hear it," replied Savana. "Do *not* marry this man! There is blood on his hands and the rest of the family," said her brother.

"No, I can't stop the wedding now. Let's just wait. I have a feeling that something is going to happen soon. I better go home now. Hurry up Jerry -let's go or Gabriele will be looking for us! Good night all!"

On a beautiful Saturday morning in the city of Sicily, the cool breeze of the Mediterranean wind blew over the shores of Sicily and the beautiful white pebbles touched the sand bringing a touch of romance. Savana and Gabriele were going to say their vows in church today. It was going to be their biggest day. They were going to become husband and wife. Savana got up very early and took a long walk down to the ocean and observed the 300-foot yacht in which they were going to have their honeymoon. Although the deck was decorated with twinkling lights and red velvet bows and the prow had a wreathe of red roses woven into a circle of green palm branches for the Christmas season, Savana did not feel too excited or hopeful. She sat down on the sand and watched the waves as they hit the sea shore. Her mind was troubled that morning and she felt covered by a dark cloud of dread in spite of the sunshine singing hope. She was thinking about Gabriele and how long she was going to have him as her husband.

He had been lying about everything to her. His past relationships and of course about Karolina. "Why is Karolina so important to him?" she wondered. She was determined that she was going to find out. As she sat there, looking at the blue Mediterranean ocean, she felt a cold hand touch her back like a touch of death. Startled, she turned around quickly and there was Gabriele.

"Good morning, what are you doing here by yourself?" he asked Savana.

"I just want to be alone before our wedding. We get married today!"

He sat right next to her and held her hands. "I love you very much and I want the best for you, and I care so much about you, my darling Savana. You are everything to me and I will do anything for you. I don't want anyone to hurt you," he told Savana. There was a pause until she spoke up.

"I have been wanting to have some time alone with you and now we are finally having that time," she said." Do you want to tell me all your hidden secrets?" she asked Gabriele.

He denied that he had any secrets and emphasized that there was nothing to hide. His heart was naked before her and God.

"Why then is Karolina being very close to you?" she asked.

"I already explained to you a while back that she knows my family. She basically grew up with them. She is like my second mother. I know Jasen doesn't talk about this but he knows."

"By the way, Savana said, I invited Jasen to our wedding and I don't know if Sophia is coming too." Gabriele was very quiet for a while.

"Does his mother know?" asked Gabriele.

"I don't think so. Jasen wants to surprise his mother and I don't want you to say anything to Karolina," Savana warned him.

"Let's go back to the house and have some breakfast with everyone," he said.

They left and Savana was walking behind him and did not say a word. Everyone was waiting for them. They ordered their breakfast right away.

"Did you have a nice walk, Savana?" asked her sister, Rose.

"Yes, I did. I was able to have some quiet time until I got interrupted by Gabriele," she said sarcastically laughing.

"Oh! He followed you to the beach? He must not trust his blushing bride," joked back her sister.

Savana did not talk or joke much after that interchange. Her heart felt heavy and she felt like being a stoic. She was very quiet. She was staring at Gabriele for a long time and he looked at her and their eyes met. He gave a long stare and he knew that Savana was suspicious about the secret he was plotting with Karolina. He said to himself that he was going to hurt Savana and her family and his family too. He could not make up his mind to do it or not. They all left to get ready for the wedding.

Jerry walked over to his mom and said: "I was looking at you earlier and you were really staring at Gabriele. I knew that he suspected that you already sensed that there were deep dark secrets."

"Son, he doesn't care if he hurts me or not. He has to follow what Karolina tells him or else. He owes her something. She knows secrets about him and his family and she is blackmailing him into silence and compliance with her every evil wish!"

"I'm not sure if I want to get married today," she told her son. "I am just going to stand up and tell everyone about him and Karolina so that they know there are secrets in this relationship."

"Mom don't do anything too foolish! Let the wedding ceremony take place and go on your honeymoon and see what happens," suggested Jerry.

Savana went with her sister Rose to get dressed in her elegant silk and pearl adorned Italian lace gown with a crown of red and white Christmas roses anchoring her long silk veil. She looked festive and so beautiful. While gazing at the flashing radiance of the diamonds bedecking the edges of her dress, her soul was drawn to the quiet pure adornment and luster of the pearls. She suddenly remembered how Christ shared the parable of the Pearl of Great Price with his followers to highlight the great love and suffering he was willing to endure for His Kingdom people. All of the events of her wedding became imbued with a deeper meaning as she experienced an open heaven for a moment that felt like an eternity.

Gabriele was at his own house getting ready as well while Savana and Jerry were at the hotel. The were not allowed to see each other before the ceremony because it could bring bad luck. Everyone was making their way to the 16th century Catholic church. There were 500 guests. Gabriele had relatives coming from Spain, France, Romania, Portugal, Greece, and Russia. In the center aisle down each pew were bouquets of fragrant red roses bound and woven with Italian lace encrusted with pearls-pearls formed by the sorrows of the sea's secrets. The aisle ended in a most glorious Christmas tree decorated with golden crosses and 30 red roses and three white roses to symbolize the years of Christ life and ministry. An antique nativity scene newly repainted in bright colors and a wooden hand- carved creche were placed under the evergreen tree, which had been brought by boat from Scandinavia. Hand dipped 12-inch beeswax candles lit the tree which was crowned with a sparkling star of Bethlehem. The air smelled like honey, roses, and spruce. Jasen and his wife Sofi and Julia and her mother as well were seated on the bride's side of guests. Gabriele was already at the church waiting for Savana to appear. He looked stunning and very handsome with his white luxury tuxedo and his red rose boutonniere. The organ music started playing Bach's *Jesu Joy of Man's Desiring* and beautiful Savana walked up the isle securely holding on to the arm of her father.

Everyone stood up when they saw Savana. For some of their guests this was their first time to see her. Gabriele could hear a collective awe like the guests were holding their breath as she walked past. Everyone whispered how beautiful Savana looked. Savana saw Jasen and his wife and Karolina. She was staring at Savana. Savana noticed that Karolina looked old and evil. The priest performed the ceremony and the newly wed bride and groom led a triumphant procession down the aisle and out of the church. They all went to Gabriele's restaurant to celebrate with an elaborate reception to honor the bride and groom. The wedding cake was beautifully bedecked with red roses. Everyone sat down while the priest said a prayer of blessing. Savana looked around and she saw the woman again was serving their food. Savana could not help it anymore; she needed to say something to her. "What is your name?" she asked. The woman did not say anything. Savana stood up and told her to come with her outside. The woman followed her outside. Gabriele was seeing all this.

"Did my husband hire you?" she asked.

"Yes, he did," she said arrogantly.

"How long have you known my husband?"

"A long time," she said with a slight smirk. Savana dismissed her and went back inside. Then Savana excused herself and left with her son, her sister Rose, and her mother. They went back to the hotel so she could change into her traveling wedding outfit.

She was getting ready to go with Gabriele for their honeymoon on their yacht. Everyone gathered on the beautiful seashore of Sicily. The cool breeze of the Mediterranean sea was blowing as the evening descended and it grew dark very quickly. Gabriele went and picked Savana up as she said her goodbyes to her family and to Gabriele's family who were now her in-laws. The boat arrived at the little quay to take them away to their large yacht. They both waved at their guests who were scattering rose petals on the beach as they stepped into to the yacht. The yacht started sailing to the unknown ocean. Savana was very quiet while Gabriele was standing next to her.

He looked back at the shore where everyone was standing and he saw them still waving at them. Finally, he told Savana they should go in now because they were ready to be served. Gabriele flipped a switch as they walked into their cabin that turned on the light in the hall, indicating that they didn't want to be disturbed. And Savana put music on the sound system in their bedroom while she waited for him. She turned in surprise as she saw him standing naked behind her, fresh from the shower, with wet hair, smiling at her.

"I have missed you for a very long time Savana. I don't like taking care of the restaurant every day without you."

She knew it was true but he hadn't asked her to come with him which meant he would be busy with meetings every day and had no time for her. She had no idea who he had met with or why he had gone and she didn't ask.

"I have missed you too all this time we have been together," she said softly her feet bare as she lay in her white satin night dress with her hair fanned out on the pillow.

He sat down on the bed next to her, slipped the straps of the dress off her shoulders, and then pushed it down her body, until she only wore a white satin thong that had been made to go with the gown. He was murmuring softly to her as he nuzzled her soft neck that smelled of roses. His body was powerful, as he let himself down slowly on top of her, pulled off the thong, and tossed it aside. He had wanted for so long to come to that day to her, and found comfort in this familiar meshing of their bodies. He always reminded her of a lion when he made love to her, when he made a roaring sound of victory and release when he came and afterward, she rested in his arms happily, and sighed as she smiled at him. They never disappointed each other and found safety and peace in each other's arms in this turbulent world. The next morning Gabriele decided to go swimming in the clear blue ocean. There were many people swimming near the seashore.

This swimming was planned by Gabriele, his new girlfriend, and Karolina. Karolina wanted to take Gabriele away from Savana. The three of them decided that Gabriele should go swimming and disappear in the water, but that he shouldn't really drown or be found dead but secretly he would be rescued by these two women without Savana knowing it. Gabriele and Savana had breakfast together and held each other and hugged each other. Savana already knew that something horrible was about to happen.

"You never held me like that before," said Savana. "It felt like this was your last hug and kiss. I never felt this way before," she said.

"I am going swimming and there are many people who are swimming near the sea shore," he told Savana. Savana noticed there were many boats too sailing nearby.

"Make sure you come back quickly. I want to go and say good bye to my parents and friends," she said.

Betrayal like the kiss of Judas was in the air when Gabriele said to Savana:

"I promise, I will come back quickly."

Karolina and his girlfriend were in this red boat. This was to be a signal to Gabriele. He saw them and he jumped off his yacht into the ocean. Savana did not see him. She waited for him for two hours. She started to get panicked and worried. She went and told the captain. They waited for another hour and he still did not show up. They alerted the police and the rescue guard and the ocean was full of police and rescue guards. Savana was crying. It was getting darker very quickly on this moonless midwinter night, but there was no place for Gabriele to be found.

She yelled out to the ocean: "Gabriele! where are you? I love you! You will always be my endless love.

Her voice echoed off into sea caves and unknown places- into the unknown ocean- full of sad memories and loneliness. Savana felt very lonely and lost.

She remembered what the priest said to her when her faith was confirmed at age 12: "The world is full of evil people and they take away precious things that are not theirs. This world is full of sorrows and ugliness. The evilness of the devil brings us sadness and ugliness, but never lose your Faith because God brings us joy in the morning."

Savana went into a deep sleep that night and woke strangely renewed in the morning. The blue ocean was very peaceful and the water was calm without a trace of Gabriele and she bravely said her last good bye: "Good bye my love, good bye my love. I will always love you until the end of time…"

She looked down into the blue abyss of the sea, she saw one floating shell, cracked open by a greedy gull, hungry for the pleasures of life, with the pearl missing- but not gone.